...from a Male Point of View

"YOU are an excellent writer. My mouth dropped at the introduction of Stony. That was so dope and unexpected." Tariq C., Georgia

"This book is really thought-provoking and extremely well-written. I enjoyed the way the author was able to tell the story in a lot of different scenarios that allow the reader to put himself or herself in the character's mind. This was truly a good read." Dewayne T., Louisiana

...from a Lady's Point of View

"I'm supposed to be doing housework but catch myself sitting up against my headboard, eyes wide open, ready for the journey ahead on each page. It's definitely a must-read, and I'm excited for what the author has in the works for us next! YaLecia L., Texas

"Stony Rhodes does a great job of bringing her characters to life and making them feel real with believable situations. I also admire how Stony is able to jump in and out of her character as herself and as a writer, diving into her character's lives so smoothly." Penny E., Florida

"...a realistic and timely tale of two people (Chase & Kendal) who were always destined for one another! Their beautiful, broken road to find one another is one so many people today find themselves on." Robin L., Texas

Advanced International Praise for the Series

@Donetta, your reaction was dead on: "Why am I crying?" (Texas)

Thanks @Elle for the feedback and outbursts of anger, sorrow, and laughter. Priceless comments: "Your book is unexpected. Not the usual telltale. I love it!" (South Africa)

Thanks @Fairytale for the kind words of encouragement: "You've truly captured the Rom-Com vibe, which I haven't seen done well in a while. I like where you started things—in medias res—and look forward to hearing more backstory. I felt bad for the actual groom, but then I re-read your summary and decided he may just get what he deserves." (New York)

Thanks @Rachael for the love and support: "Absolutely love this! Can't wait to read more. You have me feeling all these emotions! I don't know whether to cry for him or slap him silly!" (England)

A Sacred

KIND OF LOVE

BOOK TWO: *Sweet & Sour Series*

*Stony*RHODES

To be printed in the United States. This publication is not designed to provide accurate and authoritative information regarding the subject matter covered. It is sold with the understanding that the author/publisher is not engaged in rendering any marital, legal, medical, financial, or other professional service. If legal, medical, financial, marital, or other expert assistance is required, the services of a competent, professional person should be sought. This publication is also a work of fiction. Any likeness to other circumstances, situations, and/or scenarios are purely coincidental.

Please also understand that mental health is real. If you need help dealing with trauma triggers, post-traumatic shock, anxiety, depression, or any other symptoms of mental health warning signs, please seek immediate assistance from a trained—preferably licensed—professional.

Rhodes, Stony

A Sacred Kind of Love / Stony Rhodes / Fiction / Romantic Comedy

ISBN 10-digit 0-9777245-1-4

ISBN 13-digit 978-0-9777245-1-2

This book could potentially cause triggers. If you have dealt with the trauma of infidelity, please read at your discretion.

Dedication

This book is for women in relationships, who have been through some things and need a safe place to heal, to laugh at themselves, to love, and maybe even to cry, as well as to grow. Let's not be more committed to other people's happiness than we are to our own.

Acknowledgment

I read a quote that changed everything. That day I knew it was time for this story, the second story…

A Sacred Kind of Love.

To the one and only Ms. Nia Long, I thank you…

"I needed to stop thinking of what I wanted to create all those years ago and start creating what I want now."

Intro

Kendal opened the door and stood in the foyer. She took in the peace and quiet. It had been almost a month since she'd left, and now it was time to face the music. She'd gone as far as she could; Kasey, her sister, had helped as much as she'd allowed, and her mother had worked all but her last nerve over the previous several weeks. With her patient released and Terri helping with the kids, she was able to return home, whether she wanted to or not.

Setting her bags down, Kendal removed her coat and gloves. She looked around and noticed how neat everything was. *Everything's still in order,* she mused. *Guess life really does go on.*

"Kendal." Jason was surprised, yet he remained calm. He hadn't set the alarm and didn't hear her turn the lock or open the door. He'd put the kids to bed over an hour ago and had just made his rounds before showering. Stuttering, he tried to get his words out. "You... You're home."

"Yes, Jason, I am. Good night."

Kendal immediately rolled her bags and headed in the direction of the guest room. Jason quickly made his way across the room and stood in front of her. He used his body to block the main hallway, although carefully considering the impact of one blow to the wrong body parts.

"Can we at least talk?"

"We will. Just not tonight."

Jason moved, and Kendal rolled her bags around him. Her cell phone rang, and she answered, "Hi. Yes, I made it."

Kendal tried to get past Jason's slender yet muscular frame. Jason hesitated. "I missed you, Kaye."

Kendal continued to walk. She hadn't had time to miss him. From Louisiana to Illinois and back to Texas, she hadn't slowed down enough to miss anyone but her children. Her mind still raced, her heart still pounded, and her body was still numb from both shock and confusion. Chase had given her new life and something to consider that went beyond Jason. When he had touched her that morning, her body had responded. Her mind was neutral, but her heart had decided years ago. Jason was the only man she'd ever made love to, but he had betrayed her. Now, between the two of them, she hadn't yet come to terms with all that had taken place. One was the center of her joy, and the other was the bane of her belief. "Good night, Jason."

Chapter 1

Watching Kendal settle in from her trip to Chicago, for the first time, Jason experienced what it felt like not to matter. Normally when Kendal returned from a trip, she leaped into his arms. Now, she hardly acknowledged his presence, and she'd been gone almost a month—three weeks, two nights, and one day to be exact.

Jason turned off the remaining lights, set the alarm, and headed upstairs. It was apparent Kendal had every intention of staying in the guest room. He could be upset, or he could choose to be grateful. Tonight, she was home. Tomorrow, he would be too. He had worked as much as he could in the weeks gone by; tomorrow, he would not.

Stony stood to stretch her legs. She'd been on her computer for hours since leaving the girls at Spondivits after dinner. It was her mission to finish this novel and finish she would. Three new chapters in, she had no idea when she would be done and had no intention of stopping before she was. It was a three-day weekend, and she refused to not milk it dry. Not tonight and not this weekend; she would write until she had nothing more to say. A quick run to the bathroom and she would be back. Simba was asleep and she was fully awake. Tonight, she would write until she passed out. Come hell or high water, she would finish this book.

Returning, she shut off her Smartphone after sending the last message of her three-day hiatus. Jess would be busy with Richard, Carmen now had Luis, and Elizabeth was visiting her aunt a few hours away. With no one to harass or inundate her with questions, Stony would get the time she needed to focus on her writing—and she would. Cracking her knuckles, as usual, Stony began again. Breathe in. Breathe out. Clear your mind. Relax... Type...

Jason readied himself for bed and his mind raced. With the first of the year quickly approaching, he had put the finishing touches on dinner and left the oven on low. The ham, macaroni and cheese, black-eyed peas, and greens his mother had cooked had all been prepared and would remain warm throughout the night. With Kendal now home maybe, just maybe, the New Year would start five times better than this year was ending.

Stony lowered her head and raised her cup. As she thought about her characters Kendal, Jason, and Chase swam through her head. Ripples floated in the cup of hot liquid before taking a sip after she blew. Kendal was in the eye of the storm. There was peace; still, chaos raged all around her.

Like many of Stony's clients, Kendal would have to realize in her own time, her own truth. She would have to decide to die living and not live dying. One involved her and her own efforts, the other would happen whether she consented or not. It would be her call. She would just have to learn to let go of her conscious self and let her instincts be her guide. Like Stony, Kendal had ended one chapter and started another.

Slowly, she began again…

"What's wrong with Kendal? Why she acting all funny?"

Jason knew and understood, but still answered with a question trying not to be obvious. "How do you mean, Mom?"

"She's being all standoffish, barely talking, hardly speaking. Did she know we were coming?"

Disregarding another question, Jason responded as indirectly as he could. "She's been working so hard lately, Mama. I'm sure she forgot."

The truth was he didn't know if or when Kendal was coming home, so when his parents called to see if they could visit for New Year's he figured the kids would enjoy seeing them, and he needed the time. He'd texted Kendal to let her know his parents would be there after Christmas, but she'd never replied.

"Now that you mention it... What kind of wife and mother goes out of town on Christmas Eve? I know she's a doctor and all, but Kendal needs to learn how to say no sometimes."

Kendal entered the kitchen without letting on she'd heard the entire exchange. "Good morning."

"Good morning, Kendal. We were just talking about you."

I know. I could hear you, she wanted to tell her father-in-law. "You don't say."

"Yes, when are you gonna start saying no to some of these work assignments?"

When your son learns how to say no to some of his work asses. Kendal poured herself some coffee and smiled at her mother-in-law. "I'm sure that's something you need not worry about, Marsha." *I could be at home all day, and your son would still go to work and screw over me. For your information, I'm better off on the road.*

"So, how was Chicago?"

Kendal loved Jason's dad. It was his mom who had always placed her under a magnifying glass. No one had ever been good enough for her only son, but her. If sons could marry their mothers legally, Marsha would have put a ring on it when Jason turned 18.

"Chicago was wonderful, Simon."

"Well, I hope you did more than just work."

"I did."

Jason perked up. Kendal rarely ever enjoyed a business trip. She'd work and return home as soon as she could get away. "What did you do?" he inquired. As soon as the words left his mouth, he regretted asking.

Kendal looked at Jason and rolled her eyes. She hadn't planned to tell this man anything, but in the presence of her in-laws she tried to be cordial. Jason noticed the look she'd given him and took heed not to ask any other questions.

"Well, once my patient was stable, I decided to spend a few hours a day doing some sight-seeing."

"Yeah, like what?" Simon asked. "I hear Chicago can be too cold to go outside, sometimes. You're not used to that kind of weather here in Texas."

Kendal thought about the cold of the night after the basketball game. Chase had carried her into the hotel and tied his bathrobe around her once they made it upstairs. When she hadn't answered which room, he headed for his.

"It was nice enough to catch the game and grab a bite to eat."

"You were at the game!"

"Yeah, it actually made me feel closer to home."

Kendal hadn't lied. Being in the audience cheering the Mavs on was comforting. Watching Chase was equally soothing.

"Well, I don't understand why you couldn't be at home for Christmas if you were at a game," Marsha chimed in.

This woman was never going let her live down staying away for one holiday. Sure, she had missed spending Christmas day with Jason, but she'd celebrated the holiday itself with her kids and her side of the family in Louisiana. Never mind she had saved a life. Regardless, Christmas didn't have to be limited to December 25th. It was a season... The Christmas Holiday... The Holiday Season... No, she wasn't home for Christmas, but she was home for New Year's. And, if they wanted to celebrate in her home, this woman was going to have to accept that just like she'd realized she'd married an imperfect man, she'd raised an imperfect son.

"Sometimes, Marsha, things come up. If you need any more information regarding that, check with Jason."

Chapter 2

New Year's had come and gone. Kendal enjoyed being home with her kids, but she could've done without Simon, Jason and Marsha. Fortunately for her, the in-laws were loading up their car now. Unfortunately, she'd be expected to communicate with their son as soon as they drove off.

"Guess we'll be seeing you for the party." Simon zipped his jacket and then hugged Jason.

"Party? What party?"

"Dad, it was supposed to be a surprise."

"Awl, I'm awfully sorry, son."

Kendal waited. "I'm sorry, darlin'. I thought you knew already."

"It's okay, Simon. I'm sure there's still more for me to find out."

Jason felt the sting and clenched his jaw. His nostrils flared from the pain that shot through his heart. He knew Kendal was beyond upset, and he had a long way to go to restore the peace in his home, if she even gave him the chance. He figured a good place to start would be a surprise 10th anniversary party.

"So, when's the party and what are we celebrating?"

Simon eyed Jason for permission. "It's okay, Dad. She was bound to find out sooner or later. I have nothing else to hide."

Jason looked at Kendal when he made the last comment. He needed her to know there was nothing else. Kendal turned her attention back to her father-in-law who was now scratching his head.

"Well, Jason told us about the 10th anniversary party he's been planning the last couple of weeks."

"Is that so?"

"Yeah, he's going all out... Sparing no expense." Simon leaned in closer, "If you ask me, I'd say he loves ya'."

Kendal continued to pay attention to only Simon, although she heard Jason shuffling nervously in the background. "I'll see you later, Simon."

Simon hugged Kendal and waited for Marsha to say good-bye to their grandchildren who were finishing breakfast.

"There she is. Finally, we can go home."

"Alright, I can take a hint. I'm coming."

Marsha hugged Jason and told him she loved him. Then, she turned to Kendal and reminded her to think about what she'd said concerning her working so much. For the first time, she noticed the two were not hugged up and hadn't been since Kendal's return.

Marsha took a few steps backward and stood next to Simon at the door. She shifted her eyes from Kendal to Jason and back again. Looking at Simon she blurted out, "Something's not right."

"What are you talking about, woman?"

Pointing at Kendal and Jason, she stated her observation. "You two haven't touched each other since we've been here."

Jason cleared his throat. Simon lowered his head.

"Normally, I would've told you two to get a room several times by now, and you both would've said, "We have a house. We have two floors of rooms."

Marsha cringed. Every time she had to endure Kendal and Jason's public displays of affection it made her skin crawl. She'd changed his diapers and wiped his bottom, so thinking that some woman found him sexually attractive never sat well with her. She knew her son was handsome; she just didn't need to be reminded of it.

"Mother, Kendal's been working hard. There's plenty of time for that later," he secretly hoped.

Marsha tilted her head. “Since when did that ever stop you before?”

“Okay, Dear, let’s go. We have a good few hours’ drive ahead.”

Jason was relieved when Simon opened the door. He’d done his best not to let them know Kendal had slept in the guest room the past two nights. The good thing was his wife was a night owl and an early riser. Even when she was the last one to sleep, she was the first one up. His parents hadn’t known she’d gone into the guest room across the hall from them after they went to bed or had come out of it before they awoke.

“Drive safely.”

“We will.”

Simon closed Marsha’s door, and Jason waited until they drove away to leave the porch. Waving good-bye, he counted to ten before turning around. “God, give me strength.”

Jason went inside and found Kendal wiping the table. The children had finished eating and were now dressing. They’d had their time with her in the last few days, now he needed his.

“Kendal...” his voice trailed in the silence.

She never looked up. Jason took a few steps towards her, and Kendal stopped cleaning. "Don't."

He stopped and waited. She started again. She would continue to ignore him until she was ready to hear what he had to say. Until then, she wasn't there. She had already resolved in her mind he had mentally and emotionally left and come back, so she could still be gone.

Throughout the day, Kendal tried hard to maintain her sanity. It would be a long weekend before she could get back to the hospital for her usual shift and not have to look at him. While she was grateful for her break, it wasn't long enough.

"Yes, Mother, I'm fine." She paused. *"And, Jason?"* Kendal repeated. "Jason? Who cares about Jason?"

"Kendal, I know you're upset. But, deep inside, you still love him."

Lola was right. She did, but like everything else, this too would pass. "Mother, I've got to go."

"Alright. Just remember, Jason loves you."

"Jason doesn't get to love me."

"Kendal."

"No, Mother. Jason has forfeited his right to love me. I'll never let him get close enough to hurt me again. His love costs too much."

"Kendal."

"Good-bye, Mother."

Kendal ended the phone call and looked up when she heard Jason come into the living room. She knew he'd heard her, so before he could speak, she asked, "So, we're celebrating our anniversary with a party?"

Jason swallowed before rendering an answer. "Let me explain."

"There's nothing to explain. I'm not celebrating anything with you, least of all another anniversary."

Kendal stood and adjusted the mini blinds. You can also cancel our annual Valentine's reservation at Perry's Steakhouse. If you don't, I will."

Jason followed Kendal down the hallway. She entered the guest bedroom his parents had been sleeping in and started stripping the bed. He went to the other side and tried to help, as always.

"Don't."

Jason froze. This wasn't what he needed, but he understood. Kendal was shutting down and wanted to be left alone.

"You've been more distant than you were while gone."

It pained Jason to be so close, yet so far away. He hadn't even been able to touch his wife. The closest she'd come to him was passing him in the hallway the night she came home.

"Kendal, please let me explain."

"I don't want to hear it."

Kendal didn't know if she wasn't ready to speak on what had happened, or if she was just in denial that it had.

"Kendal, please."

Bundling the sheets together, she exited and went to the laundry room. Jason followed behind her. "Kendal, I'm sorry." "

Tell me something I don't know."

Kendal started the washer and turned out the light on her way out. To her he was a figment of her imagination, and she would treat him as such. He wasn't the man she had married. She didn't even know the man she had married. He was a stranger, and she owed him nothing.

Many times over, Jason tried to let Kendal know he regretted his mistakes. She walked through the house without a word. Without the sounds of laughter coming from the kids, there would be no sounds at all.

Somewhere in his heart, Jason knew he had lost parts of her he'd never get back. Kendal's heart had been broken, and she didn't trust him to put it back together. Still, he wanted to pick up the pieces and try.

Gently placing a hand on her shoulder, Jason spoke softly. "Kaye, I'm sorry for everything." For the first time, Kendal didn't move. She continued to gaze out the bedroom window. This was the first time she'd been in the master bedroom since returning home. Turning to face him, she asked only one question before walking out. "Was it worth it?"

Kendal knew things had changed the day the first email came through. He wasn't the same Jason she'd married, and she wasn't the same Kendal he'd loved. Time would heal all things, but it would never begin again. The time she'd spent away had afforded her the opportunity to think about life with him or without, loving him or not. She wasn't the same Kendal, and he would soon realize it for himself. Yes, she loved him. But she hated him just as much. She'd lost as much as he had. The only difference was she wasn't sure she wanted it back.

Chapter 3

"I never asked how you heard about my wedding," Kendal inquired of Chase.

"My parents."

"I should have known."

"Not really. I don't think they wanted to be the ones to tell me."

"Really?"

"Yeah. They'd had the 'Save the Date' card for months and never said anything. Then, on the day before your wedding I called, and Mom was looking for the invitation."

Chase remembered speeding down Interstate 20 east bound, headed for the Louisiana state line. His mom was on the cordless phone going from room to room the day before looking for something. He could hear her ruffling through papers and moving furniture.

"What are you doing?"

"Looking for Kendal's wedding invitation," she'd said casually.

"Wedding invitation? What Kendal?"

His mom had laughed at him. “Kendal Paige... from across the street. The wedding’s tomorrow, and I cannot find the invitation. Guess I’ll have to call over and ask what time again,” she’d said.

Suddenly, nothing else his mother had spoken mattered. Listening to her back then was still a blur, Chase finally admitted to Kenda. It was all noise from that point on, until she’d remembered the ‘Save the Date’ card was still on the refrigerator.

“There it is. Two o’clock at The Paragon Casi...”

“Mother, I have to go. Talk to you later. Love you. Bye.”

Kendal listened attentively to Chase’s recount of trying to get to her before she married Jason. “So, by then you knew.”

“By then I knew what time I needed to be at your door before you left for the casino. I knew I had a small window of time before you left your parent’s house. I also knew Elaina may have had my jacket, but you had my heart.”

“Chase, thank you.”

“What for?”

“For being in Chicago. For being a friend.”

Kendal could hear him smile. "You don't have to ever thank me for loving you, but you're welcome." On the other end of the phone receiver, she blushed.

"I'm glad you called," Chase broke the silence. "I've made it home from practice. Can I call you tomorrow?"

"Sure."

Kendal put her phone on the nightstand. She'd spoken to everyone she needed to except Jason. Her mother, Kasey, Terri, and Chase all knew she was home safe.

Kendal fluffed her pillows and snuggled beneath the covers. She was about to pray when she heard a knock on the bedroom door. "Go away."

Upon seeing Jason, she couldn't hide her disgust or disappointment. "I said, go away."

Jason continued towards her, and she pulled the covers around her neck. "I know, but you can't ignore me forever, Kaye."

Suddenly, Kendal was reminded of the 33,000 square feet Chase had offered. She closed her eyes and remembered where she'd put the key, as Jason sat on the foot of the bed. Resolved not to speak, she laid still.

"Kendal, I know I hurt you. God knows, I'm sorry I ever took a chance." Jason paused before continuing. "No, it wasn't worth it. There's no excuse... I can't even come up with one good enough..." He let his sentence fade. "I wish I could take it back. I wish we could start over."

Kendal remained quiet. Jason stood and walked to the side of the bed closest to her. She didn't move. Kneeling beside her, he grieved. Kendal laid motionless, until he reached for her. "Don't."

Jason grabbed the comforter in his fists. His soul hurt. Kendal closed her eyes again and told her heart to be still. He couldn't have it. No matter how much he cried, how much he explained, apologized, or pleaded, it wasn't his to have and to hold anymore.

"Kaye?" Jason spoke through the tears. When Kendal didn't answer, he pulled himself up on the bed and sat beside her. Even if she never said a word, he wasn't leaving. He'd been waiting to talk to her for days, and she had avoided him. This was the only way to get any time alone with her.

In the mornings, Kendal had been up early with the kids and had purposely stayed out until they were tired and ready for bed. She'd brought them home the last couple of evenings in time for baths and a bedtime story. Then, she'd gotten herself ready for bed and didn't come back out for the evening. Not tonight.

In the silence, Jason listened to Kendal breathe. In the reflection of the moonlight, he could see her chest rise and fall. She'd closed her eyes and hadn't opened them since. She couldn't even look at him, and he knew it.

Jason closed his eyes, but not in time to stop the tears from falling. He felt her disappointment and carried her shame. He had let her down. Placing a hand beside her, he dared not touch her again. Instead, he rested his hopes on reminding her why he loved her.

"Do you remember the day we met?" Kendal said nothing. Jason continued.

"You were headed to class and didn't realize you'd dropped a page of your notes. Had my roommate not been behind you, you said you wouldn've passed your final exam in Biology. You ended up tutoring him because he told you the notes only helped if you didn't know everything already, and he needed 'em more than you."

Jason watched Kendal fight to stop her own tears from forming. As they made their way down the side of her face, he tried to wipe her eyes. Kendal felt him reach for her and turned to face the wall on the opposite side of the room. With her back now towards him, Jason sat in silence. Still, he refused to leave.

Biting his bottom lip, Jason let a chill go through him. When that one ended, another started. Kendal had never been so cold. Slowly, he continued. He would not leave.

"When I saw you two in the library, you had just gotten out of class, so I didn't bother you guys. David later introduced us at his party. He told me then there was something different about you, and I was determined to find out what."

Kendal breathed in and exhaled. "I found out you were in ROTC. I found out you had a twin. I found out you loved music and enjoyed the simple things in life. You weren't like most of the other girls. You weren't into cars or athletes. You could care less if a guy was wealthy or had means to buy you things. You just embraced life and you loved people... and, you were so sincere. You took a genuine interest in everyone you met, including me. When most people had written me off, you believed in me."

Jason watched Kendal a little longer. "We talked for hours after leaving the party. We grabbed a bite to eat... I know you hear me, Kaye... I also know you wish I'd shut up and leave you alone. But, that's just it. I can't. I've never been able to. I asked you to the dance that night, and we've been together ever since. I went to summer school because of you. I almost got kicked off the basketball team because of you..."

Jason stopped talking and rubbed the back of his neck. He felt himself choking up. It was Kendal who had been the best and biggest part of him. When she decided to start medical school, he'd encouraged her and told her he'd wait. He turned down several job offers around the country to stay near her. He couldn't live without her then, and he wasn't about to now.

"I missed you while you were gone. We've never been apart longer than a week or so for business, but for the first time I was afraid you weren't coming home... that you'd left me for sure," Jason disclosed. "For the first time, you didn't take my calls. For the first time, you didn't answer. For the first time, you weren't here. For the first time..."

Jason cleared his throat. "For the first time, I can't touch you... I can't love you..." He pinched the bridge of his nose and squeezed his fingers together. "I can't feel you. You won't let me in... I can't feel you, Kaye... I just feel the pain I've caused you."

Jason laid across the bed in silence. He wanted to touch his wife. He could see her tears glistening beneath the stars. He'd tried to comfort her, and she'd moved his hand several times.

"I don't know what to do, Kaye. Tell me what you want, and I'll fix it. Just let me fix it."

Chapter 4

Weeks went by with Kendal becoming more and more distant. Jason no longer heard her sobbing in the middle of the night, as he laid across the foot of the bed. She hadn't returned to their room yet, so every night he tiptoed downstairs and sat at her feet while she rested.

Night after night, Jason watched Kendal sleeping, and he prayed she would give him another chance. Tonight, she wasn't resting very well. Kendal had tossed and turned several times. Jason didn't know if she simply couldn't get comfortable, or if she was just having trouble sleeping. Kendal felt Jason's presence and awoke.

"What are you doing?"

"Thinking about how lucky I am to have you."

Placing her feet on the floor, Kendal threw the covers across the bed to get to the bathroom. She ignored him all the way there and back. Climbing back under the covers, she asked him to close the door on his way out.

Jason sat for a little while longer. She hadn't agreed to him being there; he just used it to his advantage that she'd not pressed the issue yet. Having returned to work after the holidays, he'd allowed the highly anticipated release of his new client's return, bAbY FrAt, Inc., to overshadow his problems at home. Having stayed in high communication with David, he'd owned up to everything that had happened as a result of his selfishness.

"Kendal, I've learned my lesson. I know now that if it's important, find a way. If it's not, make excuses. I was making excuses for being with someone I never should've ever encountered, and I'm sorry. Now, I'm trying to find a way because you're important. You've always been."

"Good night, Jason."

"Why won't you talk to me?"

Jason was desperate. He knew Kendal was still hurting, but she had stopped expressing anger. He also hadn't seen her cry in over a week, although he could see in her eyes she still did. He wanted to help her but didn't know how; neither would she let him.

Kendal remained cordial towards Jason but wouldn't start or end a conversation with him. She went to work and came home. Terri was still there to help with the kids, but Kendal did very little to involve herself with either them or him in her present state. She hardly ate, only slept and worked.

"I want to help you," Jason admitted. "I know you're hurting."

"You can help me by leaving me alone." Kendal's voice was void of emotion.

"Kendal," Jason moved closer, then stopped. "May I?"

"Why are you even asking? You're not going to listen. So, why bother?"

Kendal wanted him to hold her, but not touch her. To touch her, but not feel her. She needed to be held but wanted to be left alone. He just needed to know she needed him, and she would never give him the satisfaction now. Besides, when she said 'go,' he came; when she said 'leave,' he stayed.

"Kendal, I realized I wanted to feel needed." Jason hoped Kendal would say she did need him, but she said nothing. "I also realized you needed to feel wanted. I took that from you. That's why you left."

Angry, Kendal sat up. "You're damn right!"

"Kaye, I love you with everything I have in me," he pleaded.

"That's a lie, Jason, and you know it." She ruffled the covers and pulled them to her shoulders again. Jason had tried to search her eyes in the darkness but found nothing. "If you had, there would be nothing left for you to give to anyone else. And, if you can't love me at my worst, then you don't deserve to have me at my best."

Jason let her words hit their mark. He deserved whatever she threw at him, and he would take it. Even if he didn't like what she said, she'd had finally spoken to him. "Good night, Kaye."

This time it was him who couldn't sleep. Jason sat upstairs in bed, longing for Kendal's touch. It had taken what seemed an eternity to get her to open up. Gradually, slowly, he would win her back. He just needed to give her time.

Kendal remained awake the remainder of the night. Her days now ran together with each one being a continuation of the previous one. There was a time when everyday was a new beginning... a new start... Now, each was a blur she wished would end. Jason had robbed her of her joy, her peace, and her will. Kasey had said it was the devil. Kendal knew the devil didn't keep her up at night; Jason did. And, she just wanted to be left alone. He hadn't been worth her heart. He hadn't even been worth her time.

Closing her eyes and trying to slowly drift off to sleep, she remembered Chase. If Jason was the devil, then Chase was her angel. He'd invited her to All-Star Weekend the last time they'd spoken. Maybe she'd reconsider. He hadn't been happy when she turned him down but understood. She was obligated to Jason; she just no longer wanted him.

Jason reached for and pulled on his bAbY FrAt tee. Being in Marketing, he had received his share of freebies, but this new brand was one of his favorites and most comfortable.

As he made his way back downstairs, Jason found a trail of clothes leading into the kitchen. Rounding the corner, he spotted Kendal swimming naked in the heated pool through the sliding glass doors. It was now 3:00 a.m., and he concluded she must not be able to rest either.

Jason stood in the shadows of the kitchen and admired his wife, sipping on the bottle of water he'd come to retrieve from the kitchen. She'd put on a little more weight, but it didn't take away from her small waist or full hips. He watched as she floated past, unaware he was there. Although he knew she'd taken on some recent insecurities, he still saw her strength.

Kendal made several laps, and Jason waited to see each one. Minutes later she climbed the stairs, and he held a towel open for her without a word. Kendal stood before Jason and looked for another option. She did her best to cover herself with her arms with little success. He could tell she was uncomfortable and wrapped the towel around her to dry her off.

"Thank you. I've got it from here."

Jason followed Kendal with his eyes. Her silhouette left him breathless. It had taken a late-night bottle of water to catch a glimpse of his wife naked. Kendal had been adamant about him keeping his distance, and he had given her space. Tonight, he regretted every stupid decision he'd made. He'd compromised his marriage and jeopardized his friendship with his wife. Kendal was his first priority and only concern. He would find a way to fix this. He had to.

Kendal walked away, picking up her clothing on her way back down the hall. Whatever feelings she was experiencing, she wasn't comfortable with them. Married almost 10 years, she couldn't remember the last time she felt awkward being naked around Jason. For the first time, she wanted to run and hide.

Kendal's phone rang just as she made her way back into the guestroom. Her heart raced as she reached for the phone and answered. An incoming call could only be an emergency at this time of night.

"Hello."

"Kendal, are you okay?"

"Yes. Are you?"

"Yes, I'm fine. I just have the most awkward feeling, and I can't shake it."

Kendal and Kasey stared at each other on their smartphones. Kendal sat on the bench at the foot of the bed and continued to dry off. Even if she and Jason had short-circuited, she and Kasey were still in tune.

"I'm okay, Kase. Something just came over me, but I'll be okay."

Not liking the sound of Kendal's voice, Kasey pried. "What happened?"

"I'm not sure. One minute I was fine in the pool, and the other I was not when Jason held the beach towel to dry me."

Kasey tapped her fingernails on the side of her face and eyed Kendal—confusion apparent in the crease of her forehead.

"I was making a few laps in the pool because I couldn't sleep. I thought he was, so I got in naked. I didn't know he was watching from the kitchen the whole time."

Kendal crossed her arms over her chest and shivered in disgust. Kasey lowered and then shook her head. She may have been the wild one, but Kendal took far more chances than she ever considered.

"So, let me get this right," Kasey blurted out as she peered into the camera lens. "You were swimming naked, and Jason was in the kitchen?"

"Yeah, watching me through the glass door. I didn't know." Kendal shivered again. "It's like ugh..."

Kasey laughed. "Girl, you are a piece of work. You know that man is watching your every move when you're home."

"No, I don't. I really thought he was asleep."

"Well, even if he was, what about the kids?"

"They *are* asleep, Kasey. Besides, this isn't about them. This is about me. I'm utterly disgusted that he saw me naked, Kase."

Kasey laughed again. "Girl, that man is probably crying right now."

"What do you mean?"

"He saw you naked and couldn't touch you. That's like throwing a steak on the back porch and expecting the dogs not to bite it."

"I don't know, Kasey. I don't remember feeling like this before. It's not like he can't see me because we're married; it's more like he doesn't deserve to see me."

"I get it, Kendal. But, do you? Jason is a man... a man who loves his wife."

"If he loved..."

"Kendal, stop. Jason loves you. I get it. You no longer feel like he deserves to get to love you. But he does love you."

"I see you've been talking to Mom."

"Not really. But I know you feel like he stole something from you, Kendal. You feel like he stole something and shared it with someone else."

"Precisely. Something I can never get back," Kendal stated. "Wait, how do you know?"

"Girl, please. All the married women I've counseled. That's right up there with feeling like there's an elephant sitting on your chest. And, you're right. You can't get it back. But, in all honesty, do you even want it back if you could get it?"

Kasey chose not to let her sister know she'd heard her conversation with Chase weeks earlier. She also hadn't been able to bring herself to ask her for details. For now, the less she knew the better. If Jason asked her anything, she wanted to be able to answer with a clean conscious. Yes, Kendal was in Chicago. Yes, she was on business. Yes, she saved another life. No sense in telling him his was about to end. As far as she was concerned, Jason needed all the time he could get to "find 100 ways" to make amends.

Kendal thought for a moment and considered Kasey's challenge. She had experienced the pains of anxiety. She'd been overwhelmed. Still, she couldn't remember ever feeling so vulnerable before now. She hated that Jason saw her. Kasey was right; he didn't deserve to even so much as lay eyes on her. To her, being naked was a badge. Being uncovered, an honor. She could be who she wanted to be… who she truly was. And, he didn't get to take that away from her. He wouldn't get to take not one more thing that was hers. Neither did she want what they had back. Maybe she wanted it better. Perhaps, she didn't want it at all.

Chapter 5

Kendal enjoyed an early breakfast with the kids. It had been a long week, and she was ready to return to work. Christmas was over, New Years was gone, and a sense of normalcy had returned.

"Lunch?"

"Lunch," Julie repeated.

"Backpacks?"

"Backpacks," the boys replied in unison.

"Okay, who's ready to tell all their friends about their Christmas?"

"Meee!" Julie's hand went up first.

"Me, too!" Caleb followed.

"Me, toooo!" Joshua announced.

Kendal smiled. Each of them had managed to clean their plates, brush their teeth, and get dressed on their own. Aside from checking their ears, pouring their mouthwash, and brushing their hair little else needed to be done. Jason had cut the boy's hair the day before, and Julie's hair had been shampooed, conditioned, and neatly styled last night.

Putting the finishing touches on her own lunch, Kendal sealed the Tupperware container and securely placed it in her lunch bag. Suddenly feeling nauseous, she pulled out a chair and rested. She hadn't slept so well, still she was expected to return to work this morning and didn't want to disappoint her team. Truth be told, she could've used the extra day to herself with the kids going back to school and Jason headed back to his office, but she hadn't spoken with anyone from the hospital since returning from Chicago and needed to be caught up.

"We're ready," Joshua yelled.

"Be right there."

Kendal stood and pushed the chair back up to the table. As she rounded the corner to meet the kids by the door, Jason met her in the hallway. "Good morning," he smiled.

Kendal told the children to zip their jackets and say good-bye to daddy. Jason followed her and helped Julie. Kneeling, he secured her hat and fastened the top button, which held it in place. After hugging each of his children, Jason stood patiently before Kendal. He waited until she acknowledged his presence and opened his arms. Closing the door behind her, she left without saying a word.

After dropping the kids off at school, Kendal headed for Baylor University Medical Center. Terri would be picking them up, with Julie being the first. Being a preschooler, she attended school only half a day, but Terri had their weeks planned a month in advance. For starters, Julie would come home and eat lunch. After a nap, she would do her schoolwork and watch one episode of her favorite show on Disney Junior. Afterwards, Terri would make sure she had a snack and some free play either in the backyard or the indoor play area upstairs. If the weather was nice, Julie was sure to get a trip to the local mall to ride the giant carousel in the food court until it was time to get the boys.

Interrupted by her phone, Kendal answered before parking her car in the reserved space in the covered garage. Grabbing her bag and heading for the elevator, she spoke.

"Hello, Mother."

"Just checking in. How's it going?" Lola asked with the sound of anticipation oozing from her voice.

"Not sure yet. Just getting back to work this morning."

"Well, have you and Jason talked?"

"Not about anything in particular."

"Kendal..."

"I'm getting in the elevator. I may lose..."

Kendal exhaled as the call dropped. The timing couldn't have been more perfect. After talking to Kasey most of the night, she didn't need to relive any of it with Lola. Kasey had been spot-on. How Kendal felt was valid. She could go back on her motives for why Jason wasn't worthy, but not on her feelings. Whatever had made her feel the way she felt could have been wrong, but how she felt would always be right.

Exiting the elevator, Kendal became lightheaded again. Taking a few seconds and hoping it would pass, she leaned against a wall when passing through the doors. *I've got to stop reliving this stress.*

"Dr. Winters! Are you okay?"

"Yes, Natalie. I don't think I got enough sleep last night."

The young woman snickered. "You and Mr. Winters at it as usual, huh?"

It was no secret that Kendal and Jason were highly romantic and extremely affectionate. Every time he visited Kendal for lunch, their public displays of affection made some uncomfortable and others blush. Kendal never hid the fact that she and Jason enjoyed one another's company. They'd hold hands coming and going, steal kisses whenever they could, and always complemented each other publicly and privately.

When she took her seat in her office, Kendal smiled at her intern. Natalie was in the second year of her residency and had joined the once happy couple on numerous occasions for birthday, holiday, and anniversary celebrations. She didn't know the ins and outs of their relationship, but she'd seen enough to draw her own conclusion. Like Natalie, Kendal knew it was only a matter of time until many others on their work team made the same assumption that she was lovesick.

"Welcome back, doc."

"Thanks, Nat. Fill me in."

Kendal walked with Natalie to their morning meeting while they briefed each other. Natalie filled her in on what was taking place in Dallas, and Kendal updated Natalie on Chicago. A few hours later, they had made all of their rounds together. Consistently working had taken her mind off problems at home, and Kendal was able to focus on something other than Jason until they stopped.

"So, tell me all about Christmas. I know Mr. Winters went all out."

You have no idea how far out he went. Kendal kept her thoughts to herself. "Honestly, we didn't do a whole lot this year. The kids and I visited my parents in Louisiana."

Surprised, Natalie followed Kendal to the nurse's station. "You spent Christmas apart? That's new."

"Yeah, I needed some time with my family."

"Well, as long as you two have been married... and happy... it must've been a good call. I wouldn't take marriage advice from anybody but you and Mr. Winters. When my turn comes, I want premarital counseling from you two."

Kendal's stomach knotted up again. She couldn't bear to tell her mentee all was not well in paradise.

"Natalie?"

"Yes, Dr. Winters?"

"Would you be a dear and check on our patient in Room 318? I'll finish up in ICU and meet you back here in 30 minutes."

"Sure. Maybe we can grab a snack."

"Maybe, but I need to follow up with Dr. Grayson's patient today."

The two went in separate directions, and Kendal stopped in the ladies' room. On the brink of a meltdown, she needed a moment to pull herself back together. Staring at her reflection in the mirror, Kendal dared not let tears fall. She would not cry again, and definitely not here.

When the bathroom door closed, Kendal leaned forward and splashed her face. The cold water sent chills through her, but she maintained her composure and dried her face.

"Welcome back. How was your vacation?"

Kendal continued to wipe her face and proceeded to dry her hands. For a moment, she froze. Her vacation had started out wonderfully. She had picked Jason up from the airport, and they'd made love under the stars at the lake. She'd spent the next morning opening her gifts and giving him herself.

Immediately, Kendal grew nauseated once more. The thought of making love to Jason no longer brought feelings of affection or memories of passion. She was now sickened by thoughts of him sharing himself with another.

"How about I need another vacation from my vacation?"

The older nurse laughed. "Yep, sounds about right."

Kendal grabbed her stomach and ran into a stall. She made it just in time to throw up in the toilet. At that moment, she was grateful for working the early shift. The bathrooms had just been cleaned, and all of the stalls hadn't been used yet. When she ran in, the toilet seat was still up, and the smell of bleach invaded her nostrils.

"Kendal, are you alright?"

"I'm fine, Ms. Sofia." Kendal continued to throw up between questions.

"Are you sure? What did you have for breakfast? Wait, did you have *anything* for breakfast?"

Kendal thought about her morning with her kids. Joshua, Caleb, and Julie had been overjoyed that she had been the one to wake them for breakfast. Taking her time, she'd eaten a bowl of oatmeal as she watched them finish their English muffins and strawberry jam with chocolate milk. They'd even shared some of her grapefruit once she added sugar.

"Yes, ma'am. I had a bowl of oatmeal and shared a grapefruit with the kids."

Kendal threw up again. This time, she no longer held back her tears. She'd barely been hanging on for days; now, she wasn't able to do so anymore. She hadn't rested and wasn't eating as much as usual. She'd been stressed and hadn't told anyone of her recent onset of headaches. She hadn't wanted Jason to see her cry again, but never intended to breakdown here. At work, she had been the hero. Now, she was a victim.

Chapter 6

Stony tossed a ball across the floor and watched Simba pounce after it from here to there and back. Having a pet wasn't something she would've ever considered before; however, she'd admitted to herself that it was a worthy decision. She enjoyed having something to look after and take care of. She also enjoyed watching the pup's displays of affection when she came home or woke up.

The doorbell rang and Simba growled. Stony laughed at what was intended to be ferocious yet sounded more like a vibrating cell phone. Walking across the living room, she led the dog to the front door.

"Who is it?"

"Special delivery for Dr. Rhodes."

Stony looked out the window for confirmation. "One moment."

She tucked the fluffy ball of fur under her arm and turned the lock. Simba perked up when the door opened.

"Hi. I'm Dr. Rhodes."

"Can I get your signature?"

Stony switched Simba to her left arm. "Sure, one second."

"All set," announced the delivery driver. "Here you go. Happy Valentine's Day."

Stony thanked the man and closed the door with her foot. She balanced an array of flowers and balloons in one hand with the Pomeranian in another. She smiled at the bouquet the florist had put together once she reached the kitchen and placed them on the counter. While she never asked for balloons, they added an extra touch.

Simba squirmed to get down, and Stony released him. Moments later, she heard him chomping and slurping near the breakfast nook. "Looks like you've got the right idea."

Stony washed her hands and opened the refrigerator, then took out several containers in various sizes. "Let's see what we have in here."

Saturday was the day she typically cleaned the icebox. The first time she'd said that Jessica had laughed so loud she'd fallen off the bed their first year in medical school. Stony reflected momentarily. She and her girls had lived through dating, marriage, and death. They'd met on the highs of college graduation and survived the lows of bereavement. Now, here she was with a puppy and a pen, literally starting a new chapter.

Simba yipped, and Stony looked down. The puppy wagged its tail and ran in circles, then scooted itself across the floor on its rear end. Bursting into laughter, Stony frightened the little creature, and it ran into the den. She continued to laugh and pulled a freshly washed plate from the dishwasher. When she placed it on the counter, Stony bit into a left-over chicken wing and grabbed a slice of bread. After knotting the bag closed, to keep the other slices fresh, she put the remaining wings on her plate and microwaved the last of the macaroni and cheese with the mashed potatoes. *That's a lot of starch.*

While the appliance beeped, Stony took another bite of cold chicken and discarded the now empty containers and returned to the fridge. She poured lemonade and prepared to consume the rest of her meal. By dinner, she'd planned to write another few chapters, but first she needed fuel for the fire. There was something about cold, leftover chicken that always satisfied her soul.

Just as Stony sat down and finished the first wing, the phone rang. Reading the name and number displayed across the television, she chewed even slower. When the answering machine picked up, Stony swallowed.

"Hey girl, this is Elizabeth. Just checking to see what you were up to this evening. Give me a call. Maybe we can catch a movie."

Stony took another bite of her chicken. "Not tonight, Liz. This year, I'm doing something different."

Stony wiped her hands and mouth, and then drank from her mason jar. Last year and the year before, she and Elizabeth had spent several hours together when Elizabeth got off work. They'd laughed and cried, then talked and laughed and cried some more.

From chick flicks to 80's and 90's music, the two had afforded one another the opportunity to grin and grieve being alone in her own way. Carmen always had a date. Jessica had Richard. This year, she had Simba. She would laugh and cry, if need be, at home. This was the second Valentine's since the only man she'd ever loved had died; yet she knew this was going to be her year to live.

Stony loved and missed Malcolm dearly, but in her heart of hearts, she knew if the shoe were on the other foot, she wouldn't trade places and come back to him. She'd lost him, but he hadn't left her. And, as long as he was still there in spirit, she really had no reason to cry. "Rest peacefully, Malcolm," Stony whispered. "Happy Valentine's Day, my love."

She showered and reflected on the last month. From Martin Luther King, Jr. weekend to Valentine's Day she'd made major progress in her story. Kendal and Jason had acknowledged where they were, now Fletcher and Faith would have to do the same.

Admittedly, Stony acknowledged that she'd been so consumed with Jason and Kendal that she preferred them over her clients. Now prepared to deal with the realities of life, she reminded herself where she and the Whittington's left off in their last counseling session. Their time together had gone especially well over the past few months. Her last meeting with Fletcher had surprised her when he admitted to fixing himself before focusing on their marriage.

Stony could tell Fletcher loved Faith, but she also knew she had needed to tell him love didn't always conquer all. Faith had endured years of not being supported. He'd gone off to work and expected her to be on duty 24/7 as a wife, mother, housekeeper, nurse, nanny, taxi driver, and chef—to say the least. Like many others before him, Fletcher had forgotten these are roles; therefore, he stopped seeing the person. Faith had disappeared, now she was fighting for a comeback. Like Kendal, with or without her husband, she would find her way.

Stony dressed and returned to her desk. This evening, she and Simba would celebrate the new year. But this afternoon, she would write. Jason and Chase were waiting, and Kendal was biding her time. Between work and her kids, she left little room for Jason. And, between memories of the past and hopes of the future, she had filled her thoughts with Chase.

Stony continued...

Having managed to pull herself together long enough to work and come home each day, Kendal stuck to her routine. She'd gotten stronger, but she wasn't better. Both Lola and Kasey had tried to convince her to talk to someone, but she didn't want anyone to know life wasn't as perfect as it had seemed. Besides, she had talked to Chase since they'd run into each other in Chicago. He didn't know everything, but he did know enough.

Recalling her earlier conversation with her sister, Kendal took a deep breath. Kasey had invited her to join her at a women's conference she'd been in town for a week ago. While she'd agreed to meet her twin for dinner, she had passed on the seminars. The last thing she needed was some old women in her business. Especially, since the conference was being held on her home turf. What she didn't need was to be recognized by some stranger in Walmart who remembered her story.

Kendal looked up from untying her shoes when she heard Jason come in. She turned her back to him and unfastened her bra under her t-shirt. Pulling and tugging until she was free, she tossed the bra across the room into the laundry basket. Jason followed her with his eyes. Momentarily distracted, he'd lost track of his thoughts.

“Did you need anything that couldn’t wait for me to come out?” Kendal absentmindedly turned around. Sarcasm oozed out of her. “Surely, you could’ve waited longer than the kids.”

Jason swallowed. He heard nothing. Kendal’s curves had captivated his attention through the silk tee, and he couldn’t hide the desire that had made its way onto his face. It could’ve been that he was simply love-deprived, but every glance he’d managed to steal gave way to his imagination. To him, Kendal had filled out even more. Her breasts had fit perfectly into his hands but, in his mind, she was fuller than he remembered. Standing before him in scrub bottoms and a plain white t-shirt, he longed to touch her but dared not even try.

“Jason!”

Jason looked up and met Kendal’s eyes. “What did you come in here for?”

He blushed and ran his hand back and forth over his head. He had forgotten the why’s, but he knew the what’s.

“Kendal…”

Jason moved a few steps closer to Kendal. “You look beautiful.”

Completely ignoring the complement, she moved around him to find her flipflops. Jason continued to stand

and watch her every move. He waited for her to enter and exit the bathroom, now wearing her favorite sweats when she returned. The last time he'd seen those, they'd made love in the Cadillac. That night had been a dream; the following morning a fantasy. It was the last good memory the two had made; the only one he had left to hold onto.

Thinking about that afternoon, Jason shifted his weight. The nightmare had begun and had yet to stop. Kendal had done very little to talk to him since then. Weeks had turned into months, and she still hadn't wanted anything to do with him.

Kendal ignored Jason as he continued to stare in silence. She had yet to confront him about the items she'd found in the suitcase; still she hadn't gotten all the details she was sure he'd left out. Somewhere between crying herself to sleep at night and throwing up at work with thoughts of him and Simoné, she had decided she didn't want to know. If this woman wanted him, she could have him. As far as she was concerned, the day he'd slept with her he'd sealed his fate.

Kendal hadn't questioned very many things in their marriage. Over the years she'd grown to love Jason as much as she had believed he loved her. Now, with thoughts of a brown-skinned brunette swimming through her head, she simply wasn't the same.

Remembering the image she'd discovered while at Kasey's for the holidays, Kendal could see a small resemblance of herself. The dark hair, the brown eyes… that was it. Jason had always been attracted to the Paula Patton and Meghan Markle types. No matter what shade of brown, he always went for his mother's features—Mulatto.

Kendal knew Jason. As attractive as these women were, whatever had drawn him to Simoné had gone beyond how she looked or what she wore. For him it was more about what Simoné had said. She could only imagine because right now she had no desire to ask. She no longer knew who he was and had begun to question her own self-worth as well. Kendal knew she was attractive; she just wasn't as attractive as a single woman with no responsibilities of her own. Whereas she had to plan and make arrangements to cover children and home, she was sure Simoné, like Chase, was available at a moment's notice.

Chapter 7

Kendal sat across from Chase enjoying a cup of coffee. He'd managed to meet her after practice for a short while in passing. He was headed home; she was headed to the gun range.

Finishing up, Chase took Kendal by the hand and offered her another cup. "I have some at home."

"You have what at home?"

"Starbucks."

Brushing off her earlier plans, Kendal smiled. "I've got to see this."

Kendal followed Chase's lead and made her way onto the highway after him. Pulling up to his estate, she was surprised by the over-sized house with the over-sized gate, and the extended driveway. While he hadn't been materialistic growing up, Kendal sensed his childhood dreams paled in comparison to his manhood victories.

Chase saw the astonishment on Kendal's face. He was simply grateful she was there. Snuggled on the movie theater sofa a few moments after touring, she tucked her shoe-less feet beneath her. It was Friday night, and for the first time she didn't have plans with the kids, and he didn't have a team event. The two had been chatting since their return from Chicago, but this was their first meeting since their painful goodbye.

"So, how are things at home?"

Chase wanted to know if Kendal was okay.

Kendal frowned. She wanted to talk about the mini-Starbucks-like bistro he actually had added on. "Jason's planned this anniversary banquet, and everyone is coming."

"You don't sound excited."

"Why should I be? He's only trying to save himself. I told him I'm not celebrating anything with him, let alone another anniversary."

Chase understood. Kendal was maintaining, but Jason was just getting started.

Suddenly, Kendal's eyes lit up. "You should come! Yes, you should be there."

Chase raised a brow. "Are you serious?"

"Yes. You should come. Mother and Dad will be there. Kasey and Hayden will be there. It'll be great. You guys are on my team."

Chase wondered if Kendal was really okay. I mean, to invite him to her anniversary party was a bit much, even for him. She sipped her coffee and smiled as if she'd realized a solution worthy of applause.

"Kendal, I'm pretty sure I don't want to be at your anniversary party," Chase concluded.

"Consider it a favor. I mean, you're my friend. Why wouldn't you come?" Chase laughed. "Maybe, because I've been in love with you since preschool."

"Exactly!"

"Kendal, what are you talking about?"

"Chase," Kendal sat up. "Nothing real can be threatened. Maybe that's what I've been afraid of."

"You're not making any sense."

"Jason wasn't real. As much as I thought he was and wanted him to be, he was not. I felt threatened when everything blew up. I felt threatened by the lies. I felt threatened by the truth. But, never in my life have I ever felt threatened by you. Well, there was that cheerleader..."

Chase looked at Kendal more intently. "Kendal, this is serious. And, I'm not coming to your anniversary party. I don't want to be around him. I don't want to be around you *with* him."

Kendal settled down and sat quietly. She hadn't considered what she'd asked until Chase summarized how it made him feel. "I... I'm sorry."

Chase exhaled. He wanted to support Kendal but couldn't bring himself to attend her wedding anniversary celebration; not when he'd tried to stop the wedding in the first place.

"Chase, I'm sorry. I didn't think it through. I just wanted you to be there... for me... as always."

Looking at Kendal, Chase understood. He didn't want to go. That didn't mean he wouldn't go. "Date and time?"

Kendal smiled. "I'll get you all the information. You don't have to come, but I'll make sure you have what you need in case you do."

"Kendal, are you sure about this? This isn't a game; this is life."

Kendal poised herself to look Chase in the eyes. "Yes, I'm more sure about this than I have been about anything in a long time."

She lowered her head onto his shoulder and sat still, a gesture she'd done as a child. No words were shared between them, as everything that needed to be spoken was said in the silence. Chase wasn't sure he'd be able to be a friend in this situation, but he would try. For Kendal, he always did.

The two friends sat in continued silence awhile longer. Chase wanted her to stay, but knew she needed to return home. Even if he didn't care for Jason, he supported whatever Kendal decided. For the moment, her decision was to be home for her family. He couldn't be upset about that. He loved her, and she knew it. She loved him, and he knew it, too. One day, somehow, things would work in their favor.

Kendal thanked Chase for his time and prepared to leave. Although they hadn't spent very much time together, she'd started to feel a sense of guilt. She hadn't done anything wrong, but something inside haunted her for being there.

Cynically, Kendal smiled. A music connoisseur, she thought about one of her favorite songs and its chorus. *I ain't thinking 'bout you. I ain't sorry.* Kendal smirked and turned to look at Chase before exiting. She paused and encouraged Beyoncé to continue in her head. She knew Chase would kiss her if she waited long enough. Pausing, she stood in the doorway.

Kendal blinked her eyes slowly, cautiously. Smiling more confidently, she lowered her bag and raised her arms. Hugging Chase good-bye, she held onto him as emotions ran through her. She wanted him to hold her, to squeeze her. She wanted to hold onto him forever but knew forever wasn't always promised.

Stepping apart, the two looked at each other. Silence seemed to be the theme of the evening. Even with no words spoken between them, conversation still existed. Chase leaned in and pulled Kendal closer. He expected her to resist, but when she held him tighter, he kissed her in one motion. Whether they had time to think or not, he had acted.

Chase and Kendal shared the kiss that had evaded them since high school. Twenty years ago, this would've been perfect. Now, it was still perfect. At least to the two of them, if no one else.

Slowly releasing one another, the silence thickened. There were no apologies spoken and no confessions made; both held their position until the other had opened their eyes.

Like old times, the two had spent several hours together, watching television and listening to music. They'd shared coffee as opposed to soda and snacked on sandwiches instead of popcorn. Kendal had made her way to his home, and Chase was even more determined to have her in his bed. She would be where she was supposed to be and not simply where she'd ended up. He would see to that. Maybe, just maybe, the anniversary party was the place to start.

Chapter 8

Jason sat in the living room waiting for Kendal to return. He'd stared at the Christmas tree still fully decorated in the corner for hours after showering and getting ready for bed. Jason looked at his watch and stretched. Kendal hadn't opened not one box from him yet. She'd oohed and ahhed with the kids over each of their gifts; she'd celebrated with them as she'd opened what each had bought her but hadn't touched his.

Scooping several small boxes into his arms, Jason walked back to the sofa. Kendal walked through the kitchen from the laundry room and noticed as he took his seat. Jason quickly stood again and greeted his wife.

"Hello."

"Hi."

"I was waiting for you. I thought we might be able to talk."

Kendal headed in the direction of the living room and turned down the hallway. She hadn't talked to him yet and hadn't planned to start any particular time now.

Jason called out to her, and Kendal slowed her pace. "Please. You've opened everyone's gifts but mine." His voice was soft and pleading.

Kendal turned around and watched Jason pick up the remaining box under the tree. The largest one, she wasn't sure how she'd missed it. "Jason, I..."

He sensed her hesitation and spoke up. "Kendal, I need to talk to you."

"Not now, Jason."

"Then, when?"

Jason took his seat on the sofa again. Moving the gift boxes aside, he placed them casually on the coffee table. With each box, he remembered what was inside. He'd planned his Christmas presents months in advance for Kendal. The first being the diamond bracelet she'd returned. He'd only given it to her early because he couldn't wait to see it on her or her expression when she opened it. Not knowing she would return it, Jason had completed the set with a matching ring, a pair of earrings, and a necklace. This year his bonus was six-figures, and he had spent five of them on Kendal alone.

Jason held the largest box and passed it to her. Kendal really had no interest in its contents but walked around beside him at his request.

"Thank you," Jason whispered.

Turning to face Kendal, he straightened his posture and cleared his throat. Kendal waited. Neither had any idea of what was to come, yet both were prepared for the worst. For Kendal, it was another apology followed by an I love you; for Jason, it was Kendal walking away. He'd tried to comfort her, and she'd pushed him away each time. Like a culprit responsible for breaking her favorite vase, she no longer trusted him to repair the damages. He'd been asked more than once to leave her alone and let her be. Still, he hadn't been able to do either.

"I wanted you to open these. It's almost Valentine's, and you haven't even inquired about Christmas."

Kendal listened. Apparently, this was why he hadn't taken down the tree or decorations yet.

"Please, open this one first." Jason still wanted his time alone with his wife to celebrate Christmas. He returned to the tree to bring the last box... the one with his name on it.

"You go first."

"Jason, this isn't really necessary."

"For me, it is."

Kendal sighed deeply. She closed her eyes and inhaled. Exhaling slowly, she unwrapped the large box with the beautifully placed Tiffany-blue bow. As she raised the lid,

Kendal couldn't bring herself to smile. Jason had restored an old wedding photo and had it printed in black and white. She looked at the sterling silver 11x15 frame and read the engraving: Never Come Up Alone.

Kendal placed the box on the table and blinked away a tear. She dared not let it fall. Jason passed her the remaining boxes and placed them in order. One after another, she revealed additional pieces of jewelry. Each reminding her of the previous one she'd returned. "Thanks, but no thanks."

"Kendal," Jason hesitated. This was something he'd had to practice since she'd come home from Chicago. Knowing when to speak, what to say, and when to say nothing were all traits he'd picked up in the midst of their crisis. Before, they'd talked about any and everything. Now, his confidence had faded. "It's not what you think. I wanted you to have the bracelet because you wanted it. I had already purchased everything; I just wanted you to have the bracelet early, so I never wrapped it."

Kendal rolled her eyes. Jason took notice. "I know you think I bought it as a guilt gift. Kendal, I didn't. I didn't buy a guilt gift because I didn't think I'd need one." He knew his words would sting, but he needed her to know he hadn't planned a coverup. He'd planned a display of his love.

Kendal stood. "Kaye, wait. I didn't buy a guilt gift because I had already purchased the bracelet, the earrings, the necklace, and the ring. It was already under the tree... Before anything ever happened! But, if I had to have one… If I need a guilt gift… Then the frame is it. *Never Come Up Alone.* That's the one I added. I needed to be reminded."

Jason took another deep breath. "Now, I need you to be reminded. Kendal, I'm sorry. I'm sorry beyond words. I'm sorry. I just want my wife back; I want my life back. I'm sorry."

He reached for her and to his surprise, she didn't pull away. Kendal simply stood still. This time, Jason struggled for air. He had no more words, only sighs of grief. Kendal had been his life. Before marriage, before kids, the two of them had shared every moment together. After marriage and after the kids, they had shared as many moments together as they could. For the first time in a long time, she let him hold onto her. For the last time, she felt it necessary.

Placing his forehead onto hers, Jason whispered, "I took you for granted. I took for granted you would always be here, always be mine, always be my friend."

In that moment, it all clicked. Jason felt weak. Now, it was his turn to be nauseated. He had hurt his wife, but he had wounded his friend. Maybe as a wife Kendal hadn't always been what he'd needed over the years, but as his friend she was always there. Thinking back, he now understood his father's advice. "If you take care of the friendship, the friendship will take care of the marriage. If you don't have friendship, you will soon realize you never had a marriage." He had a marriage. He just stopped taking care of his friend.

Kendal said very little during the entire exchange. She'd given up on every ounce of hope she may have had prior to this ordeal. She once believed she and Jason could see themselves through anything. However, now she believed if this could happen to them, it could happen to anyone. She had no advice to give anyone else, only her own internal regrets.

Now sitting in the quietness, the two tried to deal with their own sorrow in their own way. Jason, understanding his actions went beyond their wedding vows, had accepted Kendal's pleas to leave her alone and let her be; he just hadn't let her go or let her be. She was right. He couldn't fix it. She might take her husband back, but she'd never be his friend again. He may have a license to call her his wife, but there was no piece of paper sealing their friendship. He'd have to earn the right to call her friend, if she let him call her at all.

Kendal knew Jason was starting to see things clearly. For the first time, he looked away when she looked at him. It was now him who broke her stare and tried to hide his own disappointment. She also knew this was the longest they'd sat or spoken with each other since it all began. Maybe she wasn't ready for answers, but perhaps now was the time to let him know she had questions.

"Jason, I found the items in the suitcase."

Jason turned his attention to Kendal. He had silently started to open the gift left under the tree for him... the one marked 'Do not open until Christmas.' Kendal had always hidden his gifts from him in the early stages of marriage. He could never wait, so she'd learned to stash his items before the kids came along to help her.

This year, Julie had pulled out "mommy's gift" from under her bed after he tucked her in Christmas night. Squeezing her neck and giving her a big hug, Jason had left the kids to fall asleep and placed the box under the tree. It had been there until now.

"I'm not sure what items you're talking about."

Jason sounded defeated. To Kendal, he looked defeated. "When I was in Louisiana, I was looking for something in the suitcase and found a letter from her."

Jason closed his eyes. The sound of Kendal's *her* sent chills through him. The way she said it, he wanted no recollection of the her his wife had referenced, no sight nor sound of her. "I don't know what you're talking about. I wish I didn't know who you were talking about."

Kendal walked away, and he didn't have the courage to go after her. A tear made its way from his eye, and Jason sat back. Holding the item he'd removed from the package in his hand, he looked at Kendal when she quickly returned and told her thank you. He didn't need to open the container because he knew from the box it was a Rolex. It was the card that simply read *Time reveals all things; love reveals true things* that got to him. He'd waited to open the gift in her presence because he'd wanted their gift exchange to be special. He wanted *this* Christmas to be special because it preceded their 10-year anniversary. Now, the pains in his stomach increased. Time had revealed more than they ever needed to know, and love hadn't said a word.

With Kendal's Christmas shopping done by Thanksgiving, Jason knew she'd made the purchase long before thoughts of his betrayal came to pass. She'd engraved the now open watch in enough time to have it ready for him Christmas morning. *Time reveals all things* was etched on the back. Neither had known what that meant then. And, although he had purchased his items in the weeks prior to Christmas, he knew Kendal would forever link them to the time when she found out about his affair.

Kendal placed the opened envelope next to Jason on the sofa and walked away. "This belongs to you."

Recognizing the handwriting, Jason pushed the envelope away. "I don't want it."

"Don't act shy on my account. Everything is in there... the business card, the key to her place, the picture, and a gift card. It's all there. Oh, and the letter."

"Letter? What letter?"

Kendal kept walking. Jason hadn't been intrigued, but if Simoné had written a letter he wanted to know what she had said that Kendal now knew. Reading the letter aloud, he balled it up and threw it into the fireplace when he finished. The business card, key, picture, and gift card all followed. Jason became enraged. The mere fact that Simoné had put the letter in his bag was upsetting. Kendal finding it and him not knowing it was there all these months was further irritating.

Still holding onto his watch, Jason went to the guest room he knew he was still not wanted in. Kendal was brushing her hair and leaving the bathroom. From across the floor the two made eye contact, but neither spoke.

Crawling under the covers, Kendal balled into her usual fetal position. Tucked beneath the covers, she listened to Jason come closer after he turned the light off. He stood at the foot of the bed; this time more afraid to move than anything else. He knew what he needed to do but didn't have the wherewithal to do it. Kendal loved him; he knew that. Kendal liking him was his concern.

"Kendal, I'm sorry."

"Please, don't say that again."

"I didn't know about the envelope. I didn't know about the key, the picture, nothing. The last time I saw her, I told her I wasn't going to see her again."

"Before or after you slept with her one last time."

Jason swallowed. He couldn't lie; not if he wanted to save his friendship and the only bridge back to his wife. He thought long and hard.

With Kendal's words ringing in his ears, Jason heard her soul echo for the very first time. *Hurt me with the truth, or kill me with lies?* He had already hurt her; he wouldn't dare kill her. "After."

Chapter 9

Jason ended his phone call to David, as Kendal approached. "How do I save my marriage?"

"Easy. You save your friendship."

As Jason hung up his cell phone, the house phone rang.

"Hello," Kendal spoke into the cordless receiver. "Hi, Marsha, how are you?"

After a slight pause, Kendal continued. "Good to hear. Jason is right..."

"Kendal," Marsha interrupted. "What is going on? Jason has been very short with me lately. He almost never calls, and you sound different. In fact, you are still acting different."

"I'm sure Jason can answer any questions you have."

"I'm on the phone with you," Marsha contended.

"Marsha, Jason is waiting to speak with you."

Jason acknowledged that his mom had called again. He had avoided her since they'd left on New Year's. Aside from the usual Sunday call he'd made home, he hadn't reached out to either of his parents very much. Normally, Jason would speak to them two or three times a week. Now, he hardly called at all.

"Kendal, what has happened?"

Kendal eyed Jason. "Your mom has a question for you."

Kendal attempted to pass the phone to Jason, but Marsha interrupted. "Kendal, I'm asking you to tell me what's going on."

"Marsha, I don't want to speak about it."

"Did Jason have an affair?"

Stunned, Kendal froze. "What makes you ask that?"

"Because, I know crap when I hear it. Especially, since I've stepped in it myself."

Kendal sat at the kitchen counter. "What are you saying, Marsha?"

"I'm saying, that's what the men in this family do. They cheat. His dad did it. His dad's dad did it. Get over it."

Kendal fumed and her eyes stung. Her nostrils flared. "Why would you say that to me?" she shouted.

"Because, there's nothing you can do about it now. Is there? He's not beating you. You're not in danger. Get over it."

Kendal gasped, and Marsha continued. "It's done. Get over it."

Dropping the phone, Kendal stood and staggered her way back into the guest room. Closing the door behind her, she fell to her knees.

"Mom, what just happened? What did you say to my wife?" Jason had picked up the phone and watched Kendal leave. "What did you say to my wife?" he demanded.

"Calm down, boy. I told her to get over it."

"Get over what?"

"Jason, please. I figured out you had an affair after Kendal started to act just like I did when your father cheated on me. She needs to get over it. There's nothing else she can do about it now."

Jason fumed. "You have no right! No right..."

"Jason," Marsha interrupted, "Kendal is a big girl. You're a big boy. You get over it, and you move on. For the sake of the kids, you move on. Your grandparents did. Your father and I did. You and she will."

Jason let his mother's words permeate the air. He'd never known his dad's transgressions and wished he didn't now. Closing his eyes, he thought about his wife. "Mom, I have to go."

"Jason, Kendal will be okay. Give her time."

"What else did you say to her?"

"I told her this is what men do in this family. Truth is, I've been waiting. Something needed to bring her down from the cloud she floats in on."

Jason's blood boiled. "It would have been nice if you'd shared that with me sooner. I may have chosen to disappoint you. Just to prove you wrong, I may have had the strength to say no."

Rushing down the hallway, Jason nearly trampled the boys on their way to the garage after hanging up the phone. "Dad, mom says no running in the house," Joshua reminded him.

Jason ignored his sons and banged on the guest room door. Kendal didn't answer. Taking three deep breaths, he waited to enter. Kendal wasn't in sight, but he heard the shower running.

"Kendal?"

When she didn't answer, he proceeded to enter the bathroom. With thoughts racing through his head, Jason considered the anniversary party coming up in a couple of weeks. He considered the discovery of his infidelities a few months past, and he considered what his life might look like had none of this ever happened.

Jason rounded the corner and saw Kendal balled up on the shower floor. She'd allowed herself to slip off the bench because her whole body now needed the support only the floor could provide. When Jason saw her, he sobbed deeply. Overcome by his own grief, he saw the consequences of his actions before him. Like a DVD playing in reverse, he looked into the depth of this moment and saw from now until a few months ago. When he had said yes to the fruit of a forbidden tree, death came unto his wife and his marriage, and he cried.

Jason entered the shower to pick Kendal up. Together, their tears joined the streams flowing into the drain. Soaked, he turned the water off and his mind raced. He couldn't cancel the party because everything had been paid for. He couldn't un-invite the guests because all had accepted his invitation. Kendal had told him she'd stopped counting anniversaries, and he had ignored her. She hadn't made it past Doom's Day, and his mother had just made sure she never would. He had to go through with it, but he wasn't thrilled about it now. Before, it was his attempt to publicly display how much he loved her. It was also an attempt to guilt her into giving him another chance. Now, it was a reminder of everything that had gone wrong—terribly wrong.

Jason held Kendal. She hadn't spent a night in their bed since she'd returned from Chicago. Without her next to him, he hadn't slept. Without sleep, he hadn't rested.

Looking at her now, he wanted to be with her… to make love to her and wake from this unending nightmare.

Drying her off, he watched her shiver under the towel. Kendal was broken, and he was the culprit. He wanted to hold and console her—to wipe away the unending tears that had returned, but he dared not try her now. Having not spoken much since his final confession, Jason chose his words wisely. Like second nature, he spoke softly. "Kendal, I'm sorry for the hundredth time."

Jason covered Kendal in her robe and carried her to the bed. He pulled the sheets over her and then removed the wet bathrobe from himself, replacing it with a towel. Drying his own eyes, a million apologies surfaced. Kendal didn't move or answer. Sobbing into the sheets, she lost all concept of time or consciousness. Jason waited at the foot of the bed. He sat moment after moment at a loss, thankful the kids would spend another Saturday morning enjoying their time with Terri. Getting up to lay beside her, he slid one arm under her shoulders and pulled her into his arms to hold her once more. Familiarity warmed his heart. Together, they cried—her, because of his betrayal; him, because of her love.

Hours later, Jason awoke. He watched Kendal as she slept. The last thing he remembered was hearing her exhale. He knew she'd cried herself to sleep and snuggled beside her. Unaware that he had dozed off, he now attempted to remove his arm from beneath his wife who rested comfortably beside him. They'd both needed that time, even if they never admitted it.

Jason slowly slid his arm from underneath Kendal completely. In doing so, she shifted. Rolling onto her back, the bathrobe he had covered her with earlier now revealed her upper body. Jason clenched both fists and squeezed his eyes shut. Kendal laid beside him uncovered and his only weakness, her, was exposed.

Fighting himself, Jason tried to get up and leave her. He wanted her to rest and awake when she was ready, but he still needed her to see him as she had before. He needed her to see her husband, the man she'd loved and wanted for over 10 years.

With his body aching, he reached for his wife. Dead to the world, Kendal didn't move. Jason kissed the side of her face and ran his fingers through her hair. It was apparent to him she needed this rest, and he wanted her to have it. Still, he needed and wanted her too.

As he laid beside her, he rubbed her face. Blinking slowly, he took a deep breath and contemplated his next move. Would he just resume holding her, or would he attempt a kiss?

Wrestling with himself, Jason fought harder. What he wanted and needed he was sure Kendal was opposed to. He loved her enough to give her time, but months had already gone by, and she hadn't showed any signs of giving in. He knew his wife well enough to know she wasn't playing games, and she knew him well enough to know he would let her figure it out in her own time. He just hadn't been this close to her in months. Close enough to feel her without touching her, his heart leaped. Kendal was hurting, and it was all his fault. He had put her in this position, and even his mother had seized an opportunity to fire.

Jason thought about ways to protect his wife from here on, starting with himself. He knew that where she was, he had put her there, and he was determined to get her out. For the first time, Kendal's unconsciousness had afforded him an opportunity to get close enough to her for the flames to be fanned from within. She was vulnerable, and the more Jason thought about making things right with his wife, the more he wanted to show her the depths of his sorrow and the extent of his love.

Taking a chance, he silenced his fears by acting in faith. Jason rolled over and lowered himself onto Kendal. As she opened her eyes, he kissed her. Jason allowed Kendal to squirm, but he never broke his kiss. When she raised her hands to push him away, he placed his fingers between hers and held them firmly. He kissed her until she no longer resisted and gave in, then he removed the towel that covered him and the robe that separated her from him. With both joy and sadness ensuing, Jason continued to kiss Kendal until she opened like a flower. Then, he pulled her closer, held her tighter, and made love to her as if it was the first time.

Chapter 10

Chase looked at the Caller ID and hesitated before answering. "Yes, Kasey?"

"Chase, I don't know what you are doing, but..."

"Well, good morning to you, too."

Chase had anticipated this call sooner or later. He knew Kendal and her sister were close and, at some point, Kasey would get the memo.

"I'm not being funny."

"Neither am I. Good morning, Kasey."

"Good morning, Chase."

"See, painless. How can I help you?"

"By leaving Kendal alone. You promised me..."

"I promised you I wouldn't interfere as long as she was happy."

"Chase, I'm asking you. Back off."

"That sounds like you're telling me."

"Asking, telling, you figure it out. Just leave my sister alone."

Chase pondered Kasey's words. This wasn't the way he'd intended to start his week, but he'd never walked away from a challenge that didn't involve Kendal and thought now wasn't a befitting time to stop since it did.

"Kasey, I know you're concerned about your sister. So am I."

Kasey sensed a "but" and interrupted. "But?"

"But, he messed up. I told you, if I got another chance with her, I was taking it."

"Chase, don't do this."

"Don't do what? Talk to my best friend?"

Kasey could tell she wasn't getting anywhere. Chase had made up his mind, almost 10 years ago, when she'd asked him to promise her that he'd leave Kendal alone before he left the house on her wedding day. He'd honored that promise, and he was right. The clause was "if he got another chance." She couldn't stop him now. He'd earned another chance; Jason had foolishly given him one.

"At least promise me this..."

"Another promise? Gosh Kasey, I may as well be talking to her stupid husband."

Kasey ignored Chase and continued with what she considered was best for Kendal. "Promise me you'll give her the time she needs to process everything—*to heal.*"

"Kasey, Kendal has always been level-headed. She's processing now."

Kasey knew he was right. Kendal was the one who always had a plan. And, truth be told, if she wanted Jason out of it, she would plan the rest of her life around him with him still standing in the middle of it.

"Chase..."

"Listen Kase, I hear ya'. I know. I'll take good care of Kendal. We only talk when she calls, and we only see each other when she shows up."

"When she shows up?"

He'd spoken too soon. Maybe Kendal hadn't shared everything. "Yes. When she drops by, we chat, and she leaves. She's healing, and I'm not gonna lie and say I'm not glad I'm part of it."

Kasey knew her sister and Chase were playing with fire. There was no way the two of them could continue to talk and see each other without the lines becoming blurred, at some point. She wasn't necessarily looking out for Jason, but she wouldn't necessarily just let Chase in either. For all she cared, Jason had messed up royally.

Chase was simply being an opportunist. She couldn't blame him, but she didn't need Kendal making permanent decisions based on temporary feelings. Her love for Chase may have been life-long, but her disdain for Jason was just setting in. When the smoke cleared, Kasey needed Kendal to know what she had done and why.

"Hold on for a minute, would ya'?" Kasey pushed the hold button and dialed Kendal's number. When Kendal said hello, Kasey merged the calls. "Hey there, sis. I've got Chase on."

"What?" Chase blurted out.

"Kasey, this isn't funny."

"Nobody said it is, Kendal." "

What are you up to, Kasey?"

"That's what I'd like to know, Chase?"

When the two remained silent, Kasey spoke up. "Now, listen to me. Both of you are playing with fire. I know the two of you well enough to know somebody is going to get burned. Now, choose your poison because somebody is going to die. I only want to say this once, you two are going to hurt or be hurt. No sense in me making two separate calls to say the same thing," she concluded.

"Kasey, quit being dramatic."

"Kendal, I'm serious. One of you is going to end up hurt. You. Jason. Chase. Somebody is going down in this one."

"Why do you care? I went down months ago, and nobody was telling him anything to spare me."

Chase heard something different in Kendal's voice. He couldn't put his finger on it, but there was something wrong despite what was already wrong.

"Kendal, I understand."

"No, you don't. You'll never understand. You will *never* understand."

Kendal disconnected the phone on her end, and Kasey and Chase heard only the absence of her tone. "I'm calling her now. Next time, don't bother to include me," Chase warned.

Kendal let the phone ring. Despite it being Chase, she didn't answer. Focused on making it through the week, she tried to prepare herself for their upcoming festivities.

"Mom invited us to Sunday dinner. You game?" Jason interrupted.

Kendal considered her options. "Let's see, dinner with your mom today at her house, partying with your mom next Saturday for an anniversary I don't want to celebrate, or pulling the covers over my head and being left the hell alone. Humn... *Being left the hell alone.* Besides, the next thing I go to that your mother has will be a funeral."

Jason frowned. "Did you really have to go that far out?"

Kendal returned the face. "Ask me that again?"

Jason got the hint and called for the kids. In a few minutes they'd be leaving for church, and he'd be taking them with him to his parent's home. While he knew things wouldn't be magically different with Kendal overnight, he did expect some things to change since they'd been together.

Last weekend they'd made love, and Kendal had said even less than her new normal. It was as if she'd gone from loving him to loathing him. He was better off with her simply not liking him, but it appeared he'd pressed his luck. Kendal had admitted that in a moment of weakness she'd gone against her best judgment. She'd told him she never intended to sleep with him again, and he'd taken advantage of her vulnerability. Since then she hardly said anything and, like a spoiled puppy, he was on her heels every corner she turned.

Jason was growing more concerned. After making love, Kendal had bursts into tears again and rushed back to the bathroom. He could hear her throwing up and had concluded she was literally sick of him. Kendal had told him she no longer had peace. Her thoughts had been invaded day after day, night after night, with thoughts of him and Simoné. The very idea that he had touched her made Kendal sick. Now, her disgust was his to share. Just as she was haunted by his indiscretions, he was now haunted by her disgrace.

Grabbing her handbag and shades, Kendal made her way to the garage. Jason would get the children checked into children's church, and she would sit on the opposite side of the sanctuary. Today, they would visit his parents, and she would do as she had said and pull the covers over her head.

As she entered the worship center, Kendal was greeted by several members. "Hey girl, can't wait to celebrate with you guys next weekend."

Kendal smiled politely and waved. If she could, she would kill Jason and feed his body to the neighbor's dog. She just knew she'd be arrested when the dog mysteriously died a week after her husband did.

Several minutes later, Kendal was in her seat. "Excuse me. Excuse me."

Kendal looked up to see the wife of one of Jason's friends making her way across the aisle in her direction. Lowering her face, Kendal continued to read the Sunday bulletin. This was Jason's friend's wife, not her friend. She didn't even like them, and Jason knew it.

"Hey." Amber squeezed herself between Kendal's purse and another member. "I hear you guys are having a party."

Kendal looked up. "Hey, Amber. I'm not sure what you're talking about."

"Oh, it must be a surprise. Never mind then."

Kendal hadn't lied. She wasn't sure what Amber was talking about. They weren't having a party, Jason was. And, if she and her husband weren't invited it was because Jason had finally acknowledged that they were a strange couple.

Jason had often told Kendal she was over-reacting when Amber had approached them to double date. Taking them up on an offer, it was now Kendal's turn to tell him he was over-reacting when after dinner they all ended up back at home with her and Jason for coffee. Things were fine until Amber and Brad had started making out on their love seat across from them on the sofa. It was then that both she and Jason got the message; this was supposed to be a couple's swap. After that, Jason had asked them to leave.

Joking about it for days afterwards, Kendal and Jason were in disbelief. They'd never gone out to dinner with another couple and been asked over for a night cap, nor had they ever requested their own. Besides, what couple just starts making out in front of another couple in the other couple's home?

When Jason mentioned it to David, he had laughed at them for not knowing Amber and Brad were swingers. Apparently, everybody knew that bit of information but them. Shaking her head, Kendal stood when Praise and Worship began. Although she didn't feel moved on any level to do so, she participated in hopes that something would happen to break the generational curse she now found herself under. Stuck between a rock and a hard place, she could not move.

Chapter 11

Stony checked her messages after returning from the bathroom. She'd been on a writing frenzy for days—no TV or cell phone, just her dog and her Beats headphones. Even though she was home alone, there was something about having her Beats on her ears that comforted her and created more peace. When they came on, the world went off.

"Delete. Delete. Delete. Skip. Skip," Stony murmured as she pressed several more buttons. She'd catch up with the dog groomer later. She'd also have to call her mom another time. She loved that woman, but she hardly ever talked about anything. Somebody was sick; someone else had died. That was the life she lived at the senior living community she now resided in.

"Hey girl, this is Carmen. I know you're living it up in your head. When you finish this book, we're gonna have to get you a life. Luis has an uncle. I got his number. Call me. Bye!"

Stony laughed and let her thoughts take flight. "You'll be a monkey's uncle before I let you hook me up with anybody."

Seated back at her desk, she settled back in and picked up where she left off again. Writing was turning into her biggest guilty pleasure. The creativity was infinite. She could be anyone she wanted to be, anywhere she wanted to be. This was the life she'd longed for; she just hadn't counted up the cost of losing her husband to achieve it.

Taking a brief glance at the flowers and balloons she'd left on the countertop, Stony smiled. By now, many couples—happy or not—were out to dinner. Some reliving fond memories of years past and others making small talk out of obligation, each held onto some aspects of life and death. Only those who truly understood themselves could offer real love, and only those who could offer real love could offer life. Everyone else was a taker and, like a reaper, death had already visited or was on its way. This was the story she hoped would come forth—the story she prayed would shed light. Adultery equaled murder, and Grim would collect by any means necessary.

Stony set her mind back on Jason and Kendal. The man who had been gifted with his bride of choice wasn't aware of another waiting to take her by the hand and lead her away. This man, whose choice had once evaded him, wouldn't make the same mistake twice. Chase simply couldn't afford to. Knowing Kendal had his heart was refreshing, but knowing he still had hers was reassuring. One way or another, he would win Kendal over and, sooner or later, their love would conquer all. Jason had his chance and blew it; Chase wouldn't let another one pass him by.

Unlike Jason, Chase had made competition his life. Jason, on the other hand, had built his on sales. For Chase winning was a choice. For Jason it was taking a chance. One would score, and the other would attempt. One would win, and the other would lose. Jason had taken the wrong risk this time, and Chace was waiting to pounce. At this point, Stony wasn't sure who would be the victor. She was just a vessel. All she knew was both would give all they had. Leaving nothing on the table, every shot was fair play.

Laying her fingers across the keyboard, Stony waited patiently for her thoughts to flow again. It was freeing to close her eyes and inhale her next scene. One, breathe out. Two, breathe in. Three, type...

"All Star Weekend? What do you mean you're going to All Star Weekend?"

"Chase invited me to New Orleans."

"Kendal, you can't be serious. It's your anniversary."

"Kasey, the game is next Saturday. Chase can't make the party, so he invited me to the game."

Kasey held onto her silence. Chase couldn't make the party because she talked him out of it. He wasn't fully convinced he should go, so she had leveraged how inappropriate it was for Kendal's celebrity childhood friend to crash the party and turn all the attention to himself. Jason had no idea the two knew each other, so to think this man would walk in and put him to shame was absurd.

Chase hadn't cared but agreed. This wasn't the appropriate time to make their friendship known after 10 years of silence. He would have to continue to be the distant cousin twice removed from the family for now, according to Kasey. However, if she had her way, he would never see the light of day. He would remain trapped in the screen of the television forever. Kasey loved Chase—not nearly as much as Kendal—but she loved him, nonetheless. As a friend, a neighbor, and a play-brother he'd been one of the best things to happen to her growing up. But as his sister's secret, he was asking way too much. And, he wasn't even trying to remain a secret. No way, no how she could be part of that.

"So, you're planning to have your 10-year anniversary party and fly to New Orleans afterwards?"

"Why not? I never asked for a party. In fact, I specifically requested it be canceled."

Kasey listened to Kendal before responding. "Maybe because Hayden and I came to town... Maybe because Mom and Dad came to town... Maybe because your in-laws and several friends all came to town... To celebrate you and Jason."

"Jason and I aren't worth celebrating. This is all a lie, Kasey, and you know it."

Kasey followed Kendal across the guest room to the closet. She'd agreed to stay in the master bedroom for the weekend, only because Kasey and Hayden were in one guest room and her parents needed the other. Before now, she had always figured their house was too big for just the five of them. With a master suite and two bedrooms upstairs for the kids who shared a Jack 'n Jill bathroom, downstairs had rarely been used. Terri crashed in the upstairs suite when she stayed over, but that was occasionally. Now, while Hayden and Kasey enjoyed the upstairs suite, her parents used the room she'd moved into downstairs. She'd used the guest room more in the last few months than anyone had over the years.

Kasey helped Kendal carry her items back into the upstairs master bedroom while their parents entertained the kids. She'd asked the housekeeper to schedule an extra cleaning the day before. Although Jason had offered to assist, she had made it very clear this was in no way permanent.

"Kendal, can you try to enjoy the weekend with us? I know you're still dealing with a lot, but we came to see you. We're supposed to meet the girls at the hotel for lunch in a few hours, remember?"

Kendal had completely forgotten that her bridesmaids and her matron of honor had planned a luncheon with Kasey's help. This had been the first time they'd all been together since the wedding.

"Okay, Kasey. As the Maid of Honor, you're right. I'll try to enjoy the weekend. But I'm right, and you know it. The truth doesn't need explaining; it simply is. It needs no proof."

Kendal thought about Chase some more. He was real to her; Jason had been the lie. Suddenly, she questioned herself again. She'd run into her share of insecurities and regrets more than usual, lately.

"Kasey, how could I have been so stupid? I mean, I'm a reflection of Jason. Aren't I? What does that make me?"

"Kendal, you are not stupid," Kasey reassured. "Confused, maybe. Stupid, never."

"Then, how did I end up here? I mean, seriously, I never—in a million years—should've ended up here..."

Kendal's words drifted, and Kasey helped her hang the last of her clothing in the master bedroom closet quietly. With no more to do, she took a seat on the bench at the foot of Kendal's over-sized bed without answering. There really was nothing to say. She'd ended up there by trying to convince herself she loved Jason. Jason, as wrong as he was, wasn't her mate. He was simply who she'd decided to marry, and God would see to it—one way or another—that His covenant would stand, even if it never made it to an altar. That, she knew.

"Dang, girl." Kasey looked up. The mirror was a new addition. "I knew you told me you put mirrors over the bed, but to see them..." Kasey shook her head. "Keep Hayden out of here. I don't need him getting any ideas."

Kendal laughed. "This coming from a woman who had a stripper pole installed."

"It's called a passenger assist pole," Kasey confirmed.

"Yeah, if you were traveling; not if it's in your bedroom."

The two laughed, wholeheartedly. Kendal smiled. "Thanks, Kase."

Kasey returned the favor. "Anything for you. You deserve to laugh... to live and to be happy."

Kendal took a seat on the bed she hadn't touched since leaving the morning the e-mails started coming through on her smartphone. She twisted her lips and found herself in deep thought as soon as she sat.

Kasey touched her sister gently. "Are you okay?"

Kendal smiled. "Yeah, I was just thinking." "About?"

She hesitated before answering, "Chase."

Kasey raised a brow. "Chase?"

"Yeah. I miss him, Kasey. I've missed him for years and didn't realize it until I saw him."

There it was. Kasey hadn't mentioned Chicago yet. She hadn't really known how to bring it up. She'd let her sister fill her in on their conversations and had listened intently, but Kendal had skated over running into him in Chicago, so she knew she wasn't ready.

"So, is this why you never should've ended up here? Tell me about it."

Kendal looked at her sister and exhaled. She felt safe confiding in Kasey. She wouldn't judge her; besides, she knew Chase well enough to know he wasn't some random guy who had befriended her.

"When I saw him in the lobby of the Westin, I just hung onto him for life."

“Is that so?”

“Yes. He just held me back, and he didn’t let me go.”

Stony tried to stay in sync with her characters and their schedules. It may have been a three-day weekend for her, but she needed her characters to move flawlessly from chapter to chapter, week to week, month to month—and, if necessary—year to year. She’d gone back over her notes dozens of times to make sure everything went together. Now that she had caught Kasey up, it was time to move forward.

Stony began again.

“Kasey, I’ve prayed and asked God what am I supposed to do?”

“Until He answers, you wait.”

Kendal didn’t like that answer. She knew from personal experience waiting on God could be as short as right now or as long as next to never. If He intended for her to stay with Jason, she was going to need a right now answer because next to never would lead her straight to Chase.

Chapter 12

The DJ played song after song, and Jason enjoyed their guests. Kendal had been rather distant for most of the evening, but she had made rounds to every table with him as the dance floor cleared. Between 'hellos' and 'oh, my goshes,' she had perked up when greeted by old familiar faces... many of which she hadn't seen since their wedding day.

Spending several minutes at each table catching up, everyone laughed and shared their own stories of the couple's past. Some, Kendal and Jason had long forgotten; others, they never knew as their friends told of various experiences neither had been part of in the other's absence.

Kendal and Kasey had enjoyed an earlier brunch with their girlfriends. The ladies had caught up and spent time reminiscing on days long gone. Some were still single, others divorced or barely hanging on. The few who were still happy had decided to focus on themselves and had somehow managed to find a good balance between romance and responsibilities.

When the music slowed, Jason wrapped up the last round of conversations. He took Kendal's hand and she flinched. For a brief moment, Kendal had forgotten they were being watched from around the room. Beautifully decorated, the banquet hall was tastefully done with black and white helium-filled balloons floating high above the tables and chairs. With the food at the front of the dance hall and the DJ in the back, there was plenty room for the 100 guests who had flooded in to fill the black and white draped tables with red velvet accents.

Jason in his black tuxedo and Kendal in her white, floor-length ballgown, returned to the head table setup for them. He placed down the gifts and envelopes they'd been handed from table to table. Once their hands were free, the Event Planner motioned them towards the dance floor for the couple's dance. She'd moved the items to the gift table in the lobby but hadn't quite filled Kendal in on what was happening next. This was all Jason's idea, and he had kept all surprises a secret, despite his dad telling her of the initial event.

Jason squeezed Kendal's hand and led her to the middle of the dance floor as the music changed. Hearing the introduction to Jaheim's "Back in My Arms," she grew nervous. She'd heard this song for the first time in Chicago and had fallen in love with it. Dancing with Chase at the Backroom hadn't helped either, but now she was expected to dance with Jason. She wasn't even aware he knew this song, let alone anticipated a dance to it.

Listening to the lyrics, Jason held Kendal close. With each sway she grew weaker. Memories of Chase swam through her head, and she couldn't share this moment with Jason authentically. It already belonged to someone else. Just as she'd recently discovered, so did her heart. Chase was already in a place Jason wasn't privy to, and it had started long before she ever met him. Plus, at the rate Jason was going with his impromptu parties and love-making sessions, he never would be.

Kendal was aware that Jason had manipulated this situation to his advantage and many more things were probably still to come. Having already figured the evening out, there was no way she had decided she would walk in on his arm but had walked in with him, nevertheless.

Kendal wished Chase had been able to make it. She wished he was there to hold her now. Even if for a brief moment, he could help steady her feet. This was the worst song Jason could've chosen, but she understood. Even if no one else got it she did, and she knew Kasey and her mom did as well. Apparently, he understood all too well where they really were.

Jason leaned in and kissed Kendal's cheek. Once again, he took advantage of the opportunity to be with her in any way. As the chorus rolled around, Kendal became nauseous. She closed her eyes and tried not to see Chase.

She felt him. She smelled him. Breathing in and out, she wanted him to be the one holding her.

In this moment, she relived each moment on the dance floor in Chicago and let the song take her where it had taken her then. She'd wanted to make love to Chase that night but couldn't bring herself to. Tonight, she felt differently. Kendal pulled her partner closer and thought of 101 reasons not to talk herself out of another opportunity with her imaginary lover. Jason smiled. "I love you, too," he whispered.

Upon hearing Jason's voice, Kendal collapsed in his arms. Chase may have been on her mind, but Jason was in her arms. Chase had felt nothing, yet Jason had experienced everything.

"Oh, my God! Kendal!"

The crowd gasped, and Jason shouted for help. Several of Kendal's co-workers ran to her aide.

"Call 9-1-1!"

As several doctors surrounded Kendal, Jason froze. They wouldn't let him near her because one was checking her pulse and another was checking her breathing.

"Kendal! Kendal! Can you hear me?" he shouted from behind the barricade the attending nurses had formed.

Lola and Kasey rushed to his side, as Ms. Sofia started to call Kendal's name and Natalie held her hand. Both her intern and the older motherly woman from the hospital had been Kendal's closest allies at the office. One had taught her a thing or two about life; the other she was trying her best not to corrupt in the area of love.

Kendal had done well to keep both Natalie and Ms. Sofia at bay regarding Jason; however, now it may all blow up. While she was passed out, there was little concern about the couple and what the future held for them. When she came to, little might remain of the marriage they had all come to celebrate.

Kendal came to and Jason boarded the ambulance with her. Kasey and Hayden followed in their car with their parents in tow. Hayden remained close to the ambulance as they rode in silence. Hayden had been praying the entire time. Kendal and Jason had been through so much in the last few months that he couldn't imagine anything worse happening.

The ambulance pulled up to the Emergency Room entrance as Hayden parked, and everyone exited in haste. A few moments later, Jason's parents entered. With everyone waiting in the lobby, Kasey texted Terri to update the guests who had remained at the party. Although there was little of a celebration left, several people remained at the request of the Event Planner with Jason's approval. There was no sense in everyone leaving on their account when they had no news to offer at the time.

"Dr. and Mr. Winters?"

Kendal sat up on the bed and greeted her colleagues. Dr. Grayson and his intern entered with the nurse who had done all of the preliminary work minutes before.

"Well, miracles do happen."

Jason and Kendal looked confused.

"What? Can't blame us for wanting to be at the party of the year. We're on call. You're now on bed rest."

"Bed rest? What do you mean I'm on bed rest?" Dr. Grayson turned to Jason and smiled. "Congratulations and happy anniversary. Ten years married and ten weeks pregnant. I'd say that's newsworthy."

Looking at Kendal, the doctor burst into laughter. "Well, don't be so bummed about it. You're still young, you're still healthy, and you can still keep up... apparently."

Ignoring the last comment, Kendal mumbled, "Pregnant?"

"Dr. Grayson," she spoke up. "I want another test."

“Kendal, you’re pregnant.”

“But, I had broccoli at the party. It could be a false-positive.”

“It could be, but it’s not. You’re 10 weeks pregnant. We’ve given you some fluids to help with dehydration. Now, leave here and pick up some prenatal vitamins and iron tablets. You know the routine. Schedule a follow-up with your physician and, in the meantime, get some rest. Take the next week off until you get a follow-up appointment... and rest.”

Kendal laid still in disbelief. Jason took notice. Maybe this was the second chance he’d prayed for.

“I’ll see you guys later,” Dr. Grayson announced on his way out. “Maybe next time we’ll get to come to the party, and the party won’t have to come see us in ER.”

Kendal managed to smile. “Thank you,” Jason added. “Wow, Babe, we’re having a baby.”

Kendal didn’t respond. Every breath he drew in her presence annoyed her. This couldn’t possibly be God’s answer. If it was, she needed more time. Right now, next to never didn’t sound so bad.

Sitting up, Kendal placed her feet on the floor. When she got up this morning there was no way she would’ve fathomed the idea of being pregnant by nightfall. Jason was smiling wider than the parting of the Red Sea, and she was finally understanding the last few months' experiences. Every time she'd imagined Jason with Simoné she'd become nauseous. Whenever she saw his face and pictured the two of them embraced, she'd been ill and regurgitated. When she'd given herself to him, whenever she recalled giving herself to him, just the thought of being with him had all made her vomit. She thought it was all psychological, but it seems it was all very much real.

Kendal placed a hand on her stomach. A few moments later, she covered her hand with the other. Closing her eyes, she lowered her head. Fighting to hold back the tears, she lost again.

Kendal laid back down on the hospital bed and cried once more. These were not the tears of joy; they were tears of sorrow and pain. Jason had taken life from her—things she could never get back—and had shared them with someone else. He didn't deserve to share in this new one. He didn't deserve to still have what was left of her at all.

Chapter 13

Jason and Kendal rode home with only the sounds on the radio. Their family had been informed at the hospital of the new addition to the family. As hard as it was for him to see Kendal's pained reaction, Jason had rejoiced with everyone else at the blessing they'd received. His mother had even thrown her arms around Kendal and apologized. The two hadn't spoken since the phone call, but in this moment, Jason gave his mother access to his wife only after she made her plans known.

"God knows best, Kendal. He truly does," Marsha had whispered. "I'm sorry for your loss and for the way I handled it, but this is a season of rejoicing now. You see? We move on. God has allowed something new to replace the something old. You and Jason will get through this, and all of you will be better off in the end."

As Marsha ended her conversation with Kendal, Lola motioned for Jason to come to her.

"Yes, ma'am?"

"Help me up."

Jason took Lola by the hand and assisted her out of the chair she'd been resting in. He knew she didn't need his help, so he waited and allowed her to lead him.

"Jason, you know I love you."

"Yes, ma'am, I do."

"You have no more times to hurt my daughter. Consider this your warning from me and your second chance from *God* Almighty." Lola stressed. "You hurt my child again and, so help me God, you *will* go on a long business trip and never return." Jason swallowed so hard it was audible. "Sounds like you understand."

Lola walked away and rejoined her girls. Kasey was grinning like she'd been given the news herself, but Kendal was visibly apprehensive. Locking eyes with her second born, Lola greeted Kendal again with a smile. She cupped Kendal's face and smoothed her bangs away with her thumbs. She knew all too well the sense of confusion that had overtaken her daughter.

"Kendal, this is a blessing. Regardless of what has happened, this baby is a reminder of something greater still to come," Lola reassured.

Standing between his father-in-law and his dad, Jason watched the women dote over his bride. Kendal in her ballgown and them in theirs, the moment seemed somewhat reminiscent of their wedding day. Ten years earlier they hadn't been in a hospital and Kendal wasn't yet pregnant, but they were all equally joyous and equally beautiful. When he'd seen Kendal watching him from her father's arm, walking down the aisle, his heart had fluttered. Now, he watched her with tear-stained cheeks and puffy eyes while his heart sank to his stomach.

"I'm proud of you, Son." Simon patted Jason on the shoulder and rocked back and forth on the balls of his feet. "You and Kendal deserve all the happiness this world has to offer."

Jason cleared his throat and pulled himself back. He heard his father's words but remembered Lola's. God had given him a means to an end, and he would honor it and Kendal from now on. He just prayed Kendal would receive it in-kind. There was no way she would keep her distance with his child growing inside of her. This was his second chance. Kendal was a doctor and knew the importance of the father at every stage of pregnancy and birth. Surely, she wouldn't keep him cut off now.

Jason pulled into the garage and parked. Maneuvering to the other side to get Kendal's door, he smiled as he opened it. He hadn't made her sick. Well maybe he had, but he also had a little help. Unable to fight for himself, Jason relished at the thought that this little person had his back. At least that's the way he chose to see it.

"Are you okay? Do you need anything?" Jason had already started fussing over Kendal, as soon as they entered the house. "Here, sit. I'll bring you a bottle of water and your slippers."

"Jason, please. I'm fine."

"Girl, let the man wait on you. It's the least he can do since you've got to carry the child another six and half months, plus give birth," Kasey shouted from the coat closet, and then sat with them in the living room.

"Hello."

Jason answered the phone after a string of congratulatory texts messages began to pour in from the party. Kasey had informed Terri, who had told the Event Planner. When the announcement was made over the mic, congratulations echoed throughout the ballroom, and everyone cheered in a new celebration on the speaker phone.

"Yes, this is Jason Winters. Who's calling?"

Jason passed Kendal the bottle of water and took a seat beside her. Slipping off her heels, he slid her house shoes onto her feet after retrieving them from her tote. Had they been in her purse, he would've brought her the bag.

"Yes, I know Simon and Marsha Winters. They're my parents." Jason grew uncomfortable with the stranger on the phone interrupting his sacred time with his wife and unborn child. "Who did you say you are again?"

"Mr. Winters, this is Detective Adams. I'm sorry to tell you this. Both your parents were killed in a car wre..."

Jason stood and interrupted the caller. "I'm sorry, you must have the wrong..."

Jason let the phone fall. Kendal quickly caught it before it hit the sofa cushion. Watching Jason was like seeing a wet ghost pass through the room. His face was pale, and he had started sweating profusely. Never taking her eyes off of him, Kendal continued the conversation as her parents rushed to their son-in-law.

"This is Kendal Winters. May I help you?"

"Ms. Winters..."

"Mrs.," Kendal corrected, unsure why it mattered now.

"Mrs. Winters, this is Detective Adams."

Kendal kept her eyes on her husband. "Go on."

"Marsha and Simon Winters were killed in an automobile accident. Jason was listed as an emergency contact in both phones."

Kendal gasped. "No, no, no, no, no! No! They're not!" Kendal screamed. "They're on their way back to the hotel!"

Detective Adams waited. This was the hardest part of his job. "No ma'am. They were hit by an individual who was texting and driving in a head-on collision. Neither survived. I'm sorry."

"Oh my, God! Oh, my God!" Kendal cried. "Where?"

Everyone had figured out something terrible had happened and was waiting to hear what. Kendal grabbed the keys and filled them in. With make-up streaming from her face, she let her parents, her sister, and her brother-in-law know Simon and Marsha had been pronounced dead at the scene of the crime. They'd overheard the rest; the car had been towed and their remains were being taken to the city morgue.

Kendal rushed to Jason, who now sat across from them at the dining room table. He was too weak for words. For the first time, Kendal's dad spoke up, "You ladies stay here and tend to Kendal. The doctor said rest. Hayden and I will take care of Jason."

Kendal handed over the keys to her father. She held onto Jason with a heavy heart. This wasn't the anniversary she had expected. She had grieved the loss of her marriage for months, but it didn't compare to the loss of her in-laws. She had admitted hating Marsha after that last phone call, but she never wanted this to happen. Or, at least she never expected it to.

Jason let go and stood at Hayden's request. "Kendal, text me the info to the morgue. We'll check out the car Monday."

"Okay, Hayden."

She continued to watch Jason. She wanted to apologize for her outburst a week ago but need not mention it ever again. She'd promised the next thing Marsha had she'd go to would be a funeral, and it was coming to pass.

The three men left to identify the bodies, and the room became as quiet as it had been before they entered. Not one of the remaining ladies knew what exactly they were supposed to be doing, so they all did what was normal. Kendal somberly asked Kasey to help her out of her dress, and Lola boiled a pot of water for tea.

Several moments later, Kendal was lying down in the master bedroom, and Kasey was changing in the guest room. Together, she and Lola checked on Kendal when the teapot whistled.

"Kendal?"

Kendal sat up. "I'm awake."

Still numb from the shock of the earlier news, her emotions hadn't been able to settle yet. She had found out that although she felt as if she was dying, a new life was growing within her. Mixed emotions had come with that news, and hearing that her in-laws had died suddenly afterwards still shook her.

Kendal thought about Jason and how he must be feeling. Her heart broke for him. He'd not lost one, but both parents in the same night after finding out about the soon-to-be birth of a child. How could one report replace the other? How could they celebrate and mourn?

Kendal considered the cruel twist of fate this was. Angrily, she lashed out. "God, what is wrong with You?" she sobbed. "How could You let this happen? How could You let all of this happen in one night?"

Kendal continued to cry. The deeper the hurt, the louder she became. "I don't understand what You're doing up there. Why would You allow all of this to happen to us? To me?"

At her final release, she let go. Kendal cried harder than she had since the news of the affair. She had hoped things would get better, easier; however, they'd only proven to be progressively worse. While news of the baby may have been considered a blessing, what was hearing of the deaths of Simon and Marsha? Her mother had always said with every death comes new life; somehow, this just didn't seem fair.

Kendal cried for her husband who had lost his parents, for her children who had lost their grandparents, and for her unborn child who would never know either. She cried for the life of the little one she now knew she carried, even when she'd unknowingly wished herself away from the pain that had filled her nights and consumed her days. She cried for the parts of her Jason had shared with Simoné that this child would never know. She cried like she had never cried before because she now understood that when it rains, it also pours.

Chapter 14

"I love you, honey," Kasey shouted and waved as Hayden drove away. This would be the first time they'd spend their nights apart their entire marriage, but this was also the first time they'd gotten news of life starting and ending within a two-hour window, too. Not necessarily happy about having to leave his wife in Texas, Hayden couldn't be selfish at a time like this.

"I love you, too. I'll be back Thursday evening."

Needing to return to Louisiana, Hayden left Kasey and her parents with Kendal and Jason. He knew he'd need to return next weekend for a funeral, but there were several things that needed his attention during the week ahead.

Hayden thought long and hard as he made his way out of the driveway and onto the street. Making a U-turn in the middle of the road, he drove back to Kendal and Jason's. "Some things simply have to wait," he mumbled. "Kendal may need Kasey, but Kasey also needs me."

Parking the car, Hayden sat outside several minutes making phone calls. He knew church was in full swing back at New Beginnings, so he dialed the cell phones of both his assistant pastor and his best friend. Repeating the same information both times, Hayden filled them in on the events currently taking place.

"Yes, Kasey and I are still in Texas."

"No, I don't know when we'll be back."

"The anniversary party was last night. We found out the couple is expecting a baby this fall. The groom's parents were both killed in an automobile accident, and the funeral will more than likely be next weekend."

"Yes, that is a lot to digest. That's why I need you to take care of the church and you to take care of the house," he told each, respectively.

Hayden hung up and walked back into the house. Like a revolving door, Kendal and Jason had opened their home to church members, neighbors, coworkers and friends alike. Hayden blended with everyone else until Lola recognized him.

"What are you doing back here?"

"My wife needs me. Everyone else has their woman; I want mine, too."

Lola grinned. "Well, sounds like you need her more than she needs you right now. Come on... David made the announcement in the morning service. He called and let us know. Apparently, he asked friends and neighbors to give Jason and Kendal time, but you know people..." Lola nodded in every direction. Some had stopped by briefly to drop off rotisserie chickens with greens and potatoes, while others had delivered casseroles and lasagnas for the week. Somehow, Lola had become the welcoming committee, and Kasey was on kitchen duty.

Every guest was allowed to spend five to ten minutes with Kendal and Jason to avoid overwhelming the two. That was before Kendal headed upstairs to rest, leaving Jason to sit a little longer with some of the men from the church's basketball league. Between sounds of rejoicing over the baby, there were also well-wishes of sympathy regarding Marsha and Simon.

Jason sat on the sofa, still in his tuxedo pants and shirt. He'd hardly rested through the night after returning from the morgue to identify his parents. With his only family surrounding him, Jason took as much as he could of it in. His wife was due to give birth, and his parents wouldn't be there to welcome their fourth grandchild. He'd gone from celebrating his marriage to embracing the thought of a child, only to find himself fighting to believe nothing else had happened.

In his mind, Jason wanted to believe they'd left the party and gone to the hospital. Then he and Kendal had come home, and for the first time she'd let him rock her (and their unborn child) to sleep... in his arms.... in their bed. He tried to blink away the nightmare, only to find there was no end.

As if reading his thoughts, Lola watched Jason. An only child, there would be too much for him to handle alone in the coming weeks and months. This was the reason he'd wanted multiple children. It had all come down to this moment. Funeral arrangements and expenses would need to be taken care of, his parents' house would need to be packed, and decisions would need to be made regarding their final estate.

"Frank, Darling," Lola pulled her husband aside and nodded in Jason's direction. "Would you mind seeing if he needs anything?"

Listening to Jason retell the story of his parents' passing to every newcomer was too much. Kasey had interrupted his last conversation to make sure he'd eaten and had a cool glass of lemonade. No one else needed to hear the details of how Simon and Marsha had been victims of another's irresponsible behavior.

From what she knew, when the guys had arrived at the morgue, they had been informed that the other driver was in the middle of sending a text to someone; her message app was still open with a partial message displayed. As best they could tell, the woman was in town for the weekend and was reaching out to an old friend. Judging by the time of the accident and the beginning phrase of the text, the message had led police to believe the two cars had collided within minutes of the couple reaching the hotel they were staying at.

Kasey approached Jason just as her father made his arrival. "Are you okay? Do you need us to ask everyone to leave?" Kasey inquired.

"It's okay. Where's Kendal?"

"Lying down. She has everything she needs in the master bedroom. I checked a little while ago," Frank informed. "Kasey, I think there's someone else you should be checking on."

Frank pointed in the direction of his other son-in-law. Kasey saw Hayden and her face lit up. "Excuse me, Dad. Excuse me, Jason."

Kasey made a beeline for Hayden, and Jason sighed. He still couldn't wrap his mind around the idea that Kendal had been rushed to the emergency room and had found out she was pregnant and within minutes of celebrating the news, he had lost his mom and dad to a reckless driver.

Jason pinched the corners of his eyes. When the coroner had mentioned that the third body was brought in with them, he wanted to see the person who had so carelessly taken them from him and ended their own life in the process. While it was against policy, the coroner closed the drawers that held Simon and Marsha. Opening a third, the remains of a woman not much younger than him were revealed. Jason walked closer to get a better look and stopped. Overcome with emotions, he had burst into tears.

"Her name is Simoné," the coroner shared. "She was 36, never been married, no kids... except the one she lost in the crash. Darn shame. She was texting some guy named Jason to tell him she was in town and headed to her place."

Jason broke. As the coroner had continued to speak, Jason waved his arms as if to signal no more. Unaffected, the coroner went on. "The message concluded with I need to talk to you, and I miss you. We're guessing she was getting ready to hit send when she looked up. By then, it was too late."

Jason had waved his arms frantically as tears rushed down his cheeks. Becoming hysterical, he had wailed at the thought of his mom and dad dying at the hands of his former lover. Simoné was texting him when she'd hit them. This was all his fault.

Stricken with both guilt and grief, Jason sensed he had brought death to his home and had screamed in agony.

Had Simoné never happened his wife would still be happy, his marriage would still be healthy, and his parents would still be alive.

Once more, tears flooded Jason's eyes. Maybe he did need to be left alone. They hadn't had time to tell the kids about their new little brother or sister, nor had they told them the news about Grandma and Grandpa either. He still hadn't decided whether to tell Kendal the whole truth regarding the wreck. He hadn't yet made peace or come to terms with seeing Simoné lying lifeless or finding out she was pregnant. As far as everyone knew Simoné was visiting for the weekend, but the truth would haunt him forever. She was visiting to see him… potentially about a child.

Jason searched the room for anyone who could help. Catching Hayden's eyes, he walked over and spoke. After hugging his brother-in-law again, Jason relaxed his shoulders and turned to Kasey. "I'm going upstairs. Terri can assist with anything you need."

"Okay, I'll be sure to ask her."

"Have her bring the kids upstairs, please."

Jason slipped away in the distance and made his way upstairs. Kasey watched her brother-in-law and whispered a prayer of comfort and peace. Just in time, Terri walked by.

"Hi, hon." Kasey tapped Terri on the shoulder. "Would you be a dear and get the kids upstairs to Kendal and Jason?"

"Sure thing, Mrs. Nichols."

"Thanks, dear. When you're done, I need your help clearing the house out, so Jason and Kendal can rest. We don't want to be rude, but we need to start telling our guests good-bye."

With a nod of affirmation, Terri went to gather the children. "No problem, Mrs. Nichols. I understand."

Chapter 15

As if they were still on the farm, Lola and Frank awakened before sunrise. Brewing a fresh pot of coffee, Hayden and Kasey laughed at the sight of the old coffee pot.

"You guys found an antique store?" Hayden joked.

"We go over this every time you guys visit us. There's the coffee. There's the Keurig. See? Easy."

Kendal made her way down the stairs and joined them in the kitchen as laughter erupted again. Lola always traveled with a coffee pot, and Hayden always pointed it out.

"Honey, you shouldn't be up. You should've called for one of us."

"I'm okay, Dad. Jason's still asleep, and I didn't want to wake him. It's gonna be a long enough day already."

Kendal was right. They had a long day ahead of them. The week had been filled with burial preliminaries, and she and Jason hadn't had a chance to rest for taking care of her in-law's business. They'd made the two-hour drive with Kasey and Hayden to Simon and Marsha's days before to retrieve the couple's insurance policies, will, clothing, and many other what-nots that may have been considered necessary some years from now and returned. Lola and Frank had spent time with the children, still trying to explain why Grandma Marsha and Grandpa Simon could no longer visit.

"Where is Grandpa Simon?" Julie had asked Sunday morning when the guests had piled in.

"And, I can't find Grandma Marsha," Caleb had added.

Unable to manage, that was the first time of many to come that Jason had started to remove himself from the crowd gathered in his home. He had been inconsolable after returning from the morgue. Neither Frank nor Hayden had been very helpful. Frank had lost his father when he himself was 57, so his dad had lived to see 86 years of life. While Hayden still had his father, he hadn't counted on being on call as a Pastor during his trip. Yet, he was always prepared.

"Jason, I know it seems bad now," Hayden spoke as gentle as possible, "but the good thing in all of this is they didn't suffer." He parked the car and turned off the ignition. "Simon and Marsha didn't suffer."

"And, they went together," Frank concluded.

According to the coroner, neither of the three victims had survived impact. Both driving approximately 65mph on a two-way road, Highway 80 had claimed its share of lives.

"For what it's worth," Frank added, "we're always gonna be here for 'ya, Son."

All of the men understood this wasn't as simple as it sounded. There was no replacing a lost loved one; especially, not one as beloved as a parent.

"Mom, I'm thinking about leaving the children with Terri. I don't think it's a good idea to take them to the funeral," Kendal shared.

"Well, Honey, I understand your reasoning. Far be it from me to question another mother. Do what you feel is best."

Kendal was grateful her parents were retired, and her sister was self-employed. Neither of them had ever considered they'd be under one roof longer than a weekend at a time, but fate had proven them all wrong more than once in the last few months.

While there were still problems to be addressed at a later date concerning her marriage, for the first time Kendal felt thankful to have everyone close—including Jason. Death had a profound way of placing all that was still alive in greater perspective.

"Coffee?" Kendal offered. Everyone turned to see Jason.

"Yes, please."

Taking his seat on a bar stool across the counter, Jason thanked Kendal for passing him a fresh cup from the Keurig. He, too, was thankful for the comfort of home. Kendal's family had become his so long ago that they were all one.

In the last week, Jason had lost his parents but had been able to spend time with his wife. Lying next to him in bed, Kendal no longer moved his arm when he pulled her close. She no longer flinched when he rubbed her face or stroked her hair either. He couldn't tell if she was pacifying him with everything that had happened, or if this was all part of his second chance. He was glad to be gaining a child, but losing his parents was part of the deal he wished he'd had a chance to prepare for.

Lola noticed Jason's silence. He was one of the sons God had blessed her with when she gave her blessing to marry her youngest daughter, and she hadn't treated him any differently until now—almost. Lola's only ill words to Jason involved the onset of drama he'd brought into her daughter's life. But, like him, she hoped the new baby would help them work everything out. He would struggle with the death of his parents, but he would get through it with the birth of his child.

Kasey took notice of the time and reminded everyone the limo would be by to pick them all up soon. They'd ordered only one car and intended to be ready. Jason was an only child, and both his parents were only children. With no aunts or uncles, he had grown up with no cousins but lots of friends. He was the last of the Winters men, with the exception of Joshua and Caleb. They were all the family he had left now, and somehow Kasey knew he would hold on to them all for dear life. He may have let them go before, but he would never release his grip so carelessly again. Not after losing his parents, and certainly not after crushing his wife. He would hold onto Kendal as best he could, for as long as he could.

As each of the adults filed out of the kitchen, the children came downstairs. Finally understanding that both Grandma Marsha and Grandpa Simon were in a deep sleep that only God would wake them from, they still expressed their disappointment.

"I don't know why they had to sleep already," Joshua shared. "They don't want us to wake them up?"

"Yeah, Grandpa Simon always wants us to wake him up. We have to help him make breakfast," Caleb reminded.

Jason called the boys over to him, as Julie followed. Giving them a tight hug and several kisses, he told the kids a story.

"Grandpa Simon won't be making breakfast anymore because Grandma Marsha isn't here to eat it. But, you know what?"

"What?" they all asked.

"I know how to fix his chocolate chip pancakes."

"You do?"

"Yes. And, his blueberry muffins."

"Really?"

"Yes. Why do you sound so surprised?"

"Dad," Julie spoke up. "Because, you never cook anything."

Jason managed a slight laugh. "That's because your mom doesn't want you to have chocolate chip pancakes or blueberry muffins. Which is why Grandma Marsha gave them to you at her house."

The kids all looked at Kendal quizzically. "Okay, maybe on special days you can have chocolate chip pancakes."

"Yay!" they all exclaimed and rushed to hug Kendal.

"Easy. Easy," Jason warned. "You have to hug softer. Remember what we told you last night?"

"Oh yeah, the baby," Julie whispered.

Kendal lowered her cup of orange juice and hugged her children. The moment was bittersweet, but she enjoyed it best she could. Jason had laughed for the first time in days.

"Hello in there, little sister," Julie spoke.

"No, it's not. It's a little brother," the boys joined in.

Sensing the oncoming hostility, Jason spoke up. "Whatever it is, it's ours to have and to hold... from this day forward. He looked at Kendal and stared lovingly. "Whatever it is, I'm glad it is."

Kendal returned her attention back to her children. She lowered her head and felt Jason's eyes searching her soul. Looking up, she offered a smile. Jason felt Kendal's 'I love you' and let it be. He walked towards her, and they all embraced for the first time since he'd returned from his trip to Minnesota. They'd said good night to the kids and gone to bed. The next morning they'd awakened and made love.

Later, Kendal had vanished unaware she was with child. So many thoughts went through Jason's head in that moment. She had conceived the morning of the robe and bracelets, and she was pregnant when she left him on the balcony. She was pregnant in Louisiana and in Chicago.

She was pregnant both Christmas and New Year's. She was pregnant when she'd left and when she'd returned... pregnant before and after the e-mail... before and after the letter… before and after the anniversary party.

Hours later, Jason silently thanked God sitting next to Kendal at the funeral services as she held his hand. Had Kendal not found out about the baby, she may have still been distant; she may still have chosen to be short with him; and, she may have still chosen to leave him. For the first time, he had a real chance to fix everything. He just needed to get past his parents' death to see the possibility of life. Seven hours ago, he was a wreck. Prayerfully, seven months from now he would have peace.

As the service came to an end, Simon and Marsha's pastor decided to extend additional condolences:

"Before we prepare to exit, I would like to take a moment to offer up a prayer for the young woman and her unborn child involved in the crash. Although we may never understand, the Lord sees and knows all."

His words were followed by a number of 'yes sirs' and 'amens.' "We as a church are praying for the families of both Jason Winters and Simoné Clarke," the reverend announced.

Kendal looked at Jason in bewilderment. When he lowered his head, Kendal released his hand and stood.

Jason grabbed her arm and pleaded with her through a silent stare. Kendal conceded and took her seat.

While mourners moaned and hummed in response to what was seen as Kendal's grief, Kasey understood all too well the surprise her sister had just received along with the rest of them. Had she heard Reverend Baker correctly? Had Simoné been driving the car that had collided with Kendal's in-laws? All they had been told was the other driver was texting. How and when did they find out who, and when was Jason going to say something? Especially, about the baby?

Kasey had remembered Simoné's name when Kendal later shared the business card and photo. She would never forget that woman; neither would Kendal.

"Simoné killed Jason's parents?" Kasey leaned over and asked Hayden. "His parents died at the hands of his lover?"

Hayden looked at Kasey and finally understood Jason's breakdown when he had to identify the bodies of Simon and Marsha. The young woman in the other drawer... he recognized her before her name was spoken but hearing it had kicked him in the stomach.

Reliving that night, Hayden remembered the message... the text she was sending to someone named Jason that she wanted, no needed, to see and had missed him. Not wanting to respond one way or another, Hayden shushed Kasey. Kasey tapped his hand and whispered, "Don't shush me."

Hayden now fought to silence his own thoughts. *For every new life, one seems to go. But why so many?* Hayden cleared his throat, "Sometimes, life is simply too harsh," he whispered back to his wife.

Watching her sister, Kasey's suspicions were confirmed. Kendal didn't have to say a word to Jason; his conscious had already spoken. Hayden had a name, but Kasey had the pieces. Pregnant or not, this would do more harm than good. If he had only come home and told Kendal that night or the next morning, it might have bought him some time. But to hold onto it and hope it never saw the light of day is why he was her least favorite person already.

The family stood to exit the church and head to the cemetery. Kendal moved swiftly through the crowd, intentionally losing Jason. By the time he made his way through mourners and well-wishers, she had exited the bathroom.

"Kendal, wait."

"Jason, now is not the time."

Jason was familiar with this phrase. He knew if he didn't bring it up now, she would continue to avoid him for weeks on end. He also knew she would take less time moving back into the guest room.

"Kendal, I just found out the night of the accident."

Kendal let his words settle in the air. She hoped he would realize it and at least attempt to clean it up. When he didn't, she shook her head.

"That was a week ago today, Jason. A week ago today you found out your girlfriend killed your parents, and you didn't think you needed to tell me?"

"Kendal, I did. I wanted to. I just didn't know how. Okay? I didn't know how to tell you Simoné killed my parents."

Exasperated, Jason leaned his back against the wall. "I didn't know how to tell you my parents died at the hands of the woman I let destroy my wife and my marriage. Even with a baby coming, there was no nice way to wrap this one up."

Kendal remembered the other baby. "You knew? You knew, and you said nothing..."

"Yes. I mean, no. I didn't know she was pregnant. There's no way now to even be sure it was mine." Jason saw the sting of his words in Kendal's eyes and felt them in his chest, as she turned and walked away. "Kaye, I'm begging you. *Please.*"

Half of Kendal had already died. It seemed it would now be buried. Jason had admitted to never loving Simoné; still, she would always see the woman's face forever etched into her memories from the photograph, and Jason's betrayal would always be in her heart.

Life and death were now synonymous in the Winters' home. As much had been given, the same—if not more—had been taken. One baby was on the way, another was gone… A life for a life… A marriage for a roll in the hay… A wife for a girlfriend.

A curse for a curse, life had given way to death. The sentence had been decided, and judgement would be rendered.

Chapter 16

"I'm glad you called," Chase acknowledged. "I was worried about you. You weren't returning my messages or texts."

"Well, I'm sorry I couldn't make All Star Weekend; I had a lot going on."

"Kendal, there will be plenty of other games. I need you to be okay. And, I need you to want to spend time with me because you want to; not because you're running from Jason. I mean, at first it didn't matter. I just wanted you here... in my life... around me. Now, it kinda does."

"Why?"

"You're kidding, right?"

Kendal hadn't kidded in months. She knew both Jason and Chased loved her, but she understood that Chase was in love with her. Jason may have been at some point, then he wasn't, but now he was again. He was growing more unstable each day. Chase had always been consistent. Jason had proven to be fickle. It had taken a jealous work-wife to expose him. The irony was the same work-wife would prove to be more unstable than he was.

"It matters because for an extended period of time—that I never want to experience again—I needed to know you were safe. Not just physically, but mentally and emotionally as well. Plus, it bothered me that he gets to see you and hear your voice. I go to bed and wake up just wishing I could hear you breathe; something he takes for granted every day." Chase thought for a moment and reconsidered. "Well, maybe he doesn't now; but, sometimes that's the only reason I call you; just to hear you breathe."

Kendal thought for a second. That explained why oftentimes he was okay with them not saying a word beyond hello. She blushed internally, as she continued to listen.

"Sometimes, I don't mind being put on hold when you're at work... *sometimes...* because, I can still hear you breathing in the background. Even when you're talking to other people. That hasn't happened a lot lately. I didn't get to hear you breathe, and it bothered me."

Kendal twirled her pasta. "I'm not running."

"What?"

"You said I was running from Jason. I'm not running."

Chase smirked and took a sip of his water. "You do realize I know you better than I know myself, right?"

Kendal looked up. "What am I supposed to do?"

With a blank stare, Chase looked through her. "You already have the answers you seek. You know that, too. Just like I know you're ignoring what I just said."

"What do I say to that?" Kendal mused. "This isn't *Kung Fu Panda*."

Chase laughed, only because he'd taken several kids from the Mavericks kids' camp to see it as a community service initiative for the team years earlier. The first time he and Kendal had met since their kiss, laughter was a welcomed release. However, there was still much to speak on. From his perspective, Kendal needed to know he wanted her. From her perspective, Chase needed to be filled in on many things... the main one being the pregnancy.

The two quietly consumed their dinner and conversed between bites. "Kendal, you know romance shouldn't be done out of obligation, right? Or, guilt for that matter. Romance is heart inspired. Anything else is head inspired. If you, *or Jason*," he stressed, "has to think about it, you weren't inspired to do it. Your head moves you; your heart motivates you."

Kendal sighed. "And, what is your heart motivating you to do right now?"

"You really wanna know the answer to that?"

Kendal looked up. "Surprise me."

Chase slid his chair back and stood. Walking over to Kendal, he stooped down and kissed her. Then, he reached into his pocket and pulled out a Tiffany Blue box complete with a white satin bow and placed it on the table.

"This is what my heart motivates me to do… to simply love you. Your heart should be motivating you to forgive Jason and stay or to forgive Jason and move on. One or the other has to happen."

Kendal wanted to roll her eyes, but they were focused on the gift. Chase returned to his seat. "Do what you want, Kendal, but it's never an option not to forgive."

Kendal didn't want to hear that—especially, not from Chase. "How can I forgive someone I can't trust?"

"Can't or don't want to?"

"*Can't,*" she reiterated.

Chase sat up in his chair. His eyes searched Kendal for answers. She still hadn't told him what had changed, but he knew something had taken place the morning on the phone with Kasey. He could hear it in her voice.

"He's still keeping secrets," Kendal shared.

Chase stared in disbelief. This, he had to hear. The man couldn't be that foolish. But, first he wanted her to open his present.

Untying the bow, Chase invited Kendal to lift the lid. She beamed at the Interlocking Circles Pendant from the 1837 Collection in Sterling silver."

"Thank you," Kendal spoke softly. "How did you know?"

"What do you mean?"

"1837 is my favorite collection."

"Oh, that's easy. It represents you. Besides, the 1837 Collection is a Tiffany's staple. It's iconic. It's classy. It's bold. It's simple. It's elegant. It's original. It's you," Chase rambled. "One circle for me; one circle for you."

Kendal's eyes misted. This was the same guy who still knew her favorite color, favorite ice cream flavor, and favorite book. "I don't know what else to say."

"Say, help me put it on."

Kendal hesitated. She couldn't just waltz into the house with a new necklace on. Could she? Well, actually, she could. The necklace wasn't the problem; it was the giver.

"Oh, what the heck. Help me put it on!"

Suddenly jubilant, Kendal thought about the Chicago shopping spree. She'd come home with handbags, shoes, outfits, and jewelry. What was a necklace? Besides, none of this ever would've happened if Simoné had never happened. She deserved a necklace, and she deserved Chase.

Running her fingers through the circles, Kendal smiled. Chase had managed to turn everything around as always. It wasn't the gift; it was the thought. He'd taken his time finding what he considered good enough to be perfect for her.

"It's absolutely beautiful. Thank you, again."

Chase smiled. He'd managed to pull the Kendal out he needed to see... to reveal the one who was trying to hide.

"You're welcome. Now, please tell me what exactly you think Jason is hiding. Then, tell me what exactly you are hiding."

"What? What are you talking about? Hiding what? From whom?"

"Kendal, the morning on the phone with Kasey, you didn't sound right. Something had happened."

Thinking back, Kendal remembered and frowned. "I don't want to talk about it."

"Suit yourself. I was just pointing out the obvious."

"Which is?"

"You can't hide anything from me."

Kendal lowered her eyes. How could she tell him the morning in question she and Jason had been together? She wasn't even convinced they'd made love. They'd just *been* together.

Kendal raised her eyes and spoke. "The night of the anniversary party, I was rushed to ER."

"Wait. What?"

"I was dehydrated and stressed... I was confused and scared... pregnant and angry. One minute I was dancing with you in my head; the next I was passing out in Jason's arms."

Kendal proceeded to tell Chase how she'd found out she was 10 weeks pregnant a month ago. She filled him in on leaving the hospital and her in-laws being killed in a car wreck hours later. Chase listened in astonishment but hid his confusion and disappointment. He knew this changed things. She would never leave Jason now. Even if she never let him touch her again, she would stay for the sake of this child and this child alone.

"Kendal, I'm sorry. I didn't know. I wouldn've kept calling had I known."

"It's okay. I knew you were concerned. There were just so many people around the clock. We went from having a party to planning a funeral, and that still isn't the worst."

"How can it be any worse than what you've just shared?"

Chase tried to keep the conversation moving to not have to hear more about the pregnancy. Kendal took notice and continued. He wasn't ready to talk about it, and she wasn't ready to deal with it.

"Jason didn't tell me his ex-lover ran into his parents."

"Excuse me." Chase choked on his water and coughed. He shook his head like he hadn't heard Kendal correctly.

"The woman Jason was sleeping with was back in town for the weekend. She was texting Jason to tell him she missed him and wanted to see him... Obviously to tell him about the baby..."

Kendal's words faded and returned. "Distracted from the road, she ran into his parents on their way back to their hotel room. All four died upon impact."

"Kendal, if Jason didn't tell you how did you find out?"

"Brace yourself for this one… The preacher prayed for my family and the family of the young lady and her unborn child who had been killed in the other car."

Chase frowned. He wrapped his mind around the idea that Jason's lover had died texting Simon and Marsha Winters' only son, Jason Winters. And, he let Kendal find out at the funeral.

"Jesus, Kendal, the minister shared all that?"

"No, we knew they'd been hit by someone texting and driving. Jason was the only one who knew it was Simoné. The preacher was clueless."

Instantly concerned about Kendal's well-being again, Chase reached across the table and took her hand. "How are you holding up?"

"By thinking about you."

Although flattered, that wasn't the answer he was looking for.

"Kendal, I'm asking, what are you gonna do?"

"All I know is you can't give what you don't have, and I don't have any forgiveness... not for him."

Chase frowned. "That was rather rushed and very easy."

"Look, I don't know what you want me to say. In the last few months, I've discovered my husband had an affair, ran into the man I had to admit is the love of my life through clenched teeth, found out I'm pregnant, and buried my in-laws. A month ago, I wanted to leave him. Now, I have to leave you," Kendal blurted out.

Emotions ran through Chase like electricity. She'd known it and admitted it. If only it was 10 years earlier and she wasn't married, pregnant, or grieving. Chase sat back and sighed once more. "Kendal, you can't make this about me."

"What is that supposed to mean?"

"It means, you've got to work this out within yourself. I don't know what you're going to do. I just know when you call me, I'll be waiting. But, until then, you can't renege on how you feel."

"Renege?"

"Yes, renege. You can go back on what made you feel what you felt, but how you felt is always true... first, last, and with finality. If you aren't feeling him, you can't make yourself start. It starts in here." Chase pointed at his heart. "Mine begins and ends with you. My feelings have always been about you."

Chase cleared his throat and sat straight up in the chair. He wanted to hold her now. For fear this might be the last time, he motioned for the waiter to pay the tab. While they waited, he tried to separate his feelings for his friend from the love of his life.

“Kendal, regardless of what has happened, you have no reason to feel bad. I have illegitimate expectations that have to stop. You don’t owe me anything, least of all time.”

Chase stood when the waiter returned with his credit card and receipt. He grabbed the Tiffany’s box and ribbon and passed them both to Kendal. Centering the necklace around her neck, he stopped himself from touching her now and motioned for the door.

Following her to her car, Chase stood and waited for Kendal to place her items onto the passenger seat. After several moments of silence, she spoke. “What are you trying to say?”

Chase grabbed Kendal and pulled her into his arms. He rested his chin on top of her head and closed his eyes. Holding her tightly, he waited to let go. He could feel the bump under her jacket that he hadn’t noticed at the table. He had seen the fullness of her face and the glow of her skin but hadn’t equated it to a new life growing inside of her.

A tad bit jealous, Chase had taken in Kendal’s confession. She’d planned to leave Jason, now she needed to leave him. He was right; the answers she sought, she already had. Even if she hadn’t said it, she’d already decided.

Trying to make light of the situation, Chase asked playfully. "So, how does one break up with the best non-girlfriend, girlfriend one's never had?"

"That's not funny," Kendal mumbled under the weight of his shoulders.

"No, but just like I've set my goal and standards high, I need you to do the same. I'm expecting you to succeed at life, Kendal—not just in life. Do you understand?"

Kendal nodded, slowly. She knew what he was saying. Chase wanted what was best for her, even if it wasn't him. If she and Jason could keep it together, it would be worth it for him to walk away. If they couldn't, he knew she'd be okay. She just wouldn't be happy. That would hurt him more than anything.

Chase helped Kendal into her SUV and watched her drive away. He was glad he'd purchased the necklace. Although he'd won MVP status from the All-Star game and his wallet was full, his heart was broken, and his spirit was empty.

With a heavy heart, Chase exited the parking lot as his phone vibrated and the dashboard lit up.

"Hello."

"Why did you let me go so easily?"

"I didn't. I gave you two rings, one for you and one for me."

"You came prepared to say good-bye?"

"Who competes with Jesus, Kendal? He can give you a bouquet of stars... a field of flowers... He can give you the world, literally. Me, I can only take it away. I don't want to take anything from you. I want you to choose me, but I need you to choose Him."

Kendal's heart melted with every word, even though she couldn't verbalize or express the same sentiment without breaking down. "I love you, because I trust you," she revealed.

"You will always be the star in all my dreams," he replied. "I love you, too. "

"Good-bye, Chase."

"Good-bye, Kendal."

Chapter 17

"I'm glad you changed your mind and decided to join me." Kasey welcomed Kendal into her home and poured two jars of sweet tea. "You look good, girl."

Kendal wobbled to the sofa and plopped down. In the middle of her second trimester, she knew her days of traveling would be winding down prior to her third. She'd managed to stay upbeat and keep working, still she hadn't yet mastered her emotions.

"Yeah, well, I figured I'd better use the little time I have left to get out. Once the baby comes, I'm home for a while."

"So, tell me, how are things going between you and Jason?"

Kendal rolled her eyes. "I stay to give my kids the best life possible. The best of everything."

"Why not give them the best of you?"

Kendal stood. "I need to go to the bathroom. How much longer until we're ready to go?"

Kasey, fully aware her sister had ignored her, didn't bother to respond.

Kendal flushed and washed her hands. “Are you ready yet?” she asked exiting the bathroom.

“Kendal, when was the last time you spoke to Chase?”

“Don’t see why that matters now. Two, maybe three months.”

Kendal wasn’t sure why Kasey expected her to answer any of her questions when she was ignoring her own. The secret was out; she loved Chase, but she was obligated to Jason.

“We have a few minutes before Mother arrives. Have a seat.”

“Mom is coming, too? Oh, Lord, y’all are hell-bent on torturing me, aren’t you?”

Kasey chuckled. “No, we’re heaven-bent on spending some quality time with you while you’re here for the weekend. Is that okay with you, dear sister?”

“I guess,” Kendal replied nonchalantly.

While waiting for Lola to make the two-hour drive to her home, Kasey considered it a blessing to spend time alone with her sister. They hadn’t seen each other since the weekend of the non-anniversary anniversary party and Simon and Marsha’s home-going service, and plenty had changed since then.

"Kendal, does Jason know about Chase yet?" Lola laughed at Kasey, as she made her entrance in through the back door. "Girl, you need to miss a few of these conferences you keep inviting us to. A woman never tells anybody about her first love. And many times, it's not the one everyone thinks it is. It's the one nobody ever heard of or knew about," Lola said while having a *Titanic* moment.

"Mama, Kasey gasped. What are you saying?"

Lola smiled and allowed Kasey to help her to her seat. "I'm saying a woman never tells her last love about her first one. He may hear about others before him; but, it's not the one she tells him about. It's the one he never knew about... and vice versa." She smiled at her memories and sipped the tea Kasey had placed beside her on the coffee table.

Kendal watched her mother and marveled at the wisdom she harbored. "Mama, I don't know how you do it."

"Do what?"

Lola knew Kendal was still torn between Jason and Chase. One was her past, the other her future. One was here now, and the other was her later.

"I see you're still struggling to free yourself from the grasp of your own cocoon." Lola took another sip of her tea. "Sooner or later, your wings will be ready. Just keep struggling; it builds character. You stop struggling... you potentially die."

"Mother, what are you doing?" Kasey whispered.

Lola looked at Kendal. Nodding her head, she spoke. "She will have to realize, in her own time, the only thing she's ever been sure of in her whole life is Chase. Maybe this baby will help her figure it out."

"And, how exactly is that supposed to work?" Kendal wanted to know.

"If that baby stops moving, you know there is a problem. Don't you?"

"Yes."

"Well, if you stop moving, so will I. You chose Jason. God chose Chase."

"Some help the two of you are. Are we ready now?"

Kasey took a deep breath. She was preparing for the remainder of the afternoon speaking to another women's group at a local church. For the first time, both Lola and Kendal were free to join her.

Kasey looked back and forth from her mother to her sister. "Kendal, God is not being glorified if you're staying out of obligation. He loves a *cheerful* giver. That doesn't just speak to finances or service; it also speaks to marriage and romance. God doesn't bless mess, and many marriages are operating under the blessing until shit hits the fan, and you wake up and see it for the curse it really is."

Kendal shook her head. Leave it to Kasey to go rogue. "You are the most savage first lady I've ever known."

Lola agreed with Kendal *and* Kasey. "Well, I wouldn't put it that way," Lola chimed in, "but, God isn't in the save a marriage business if it was never in His will to begin with. Again, you chose Jason. God chose Chase. Chase has always been the one, even when you didn't want him to be."

This time it was Kasey who frowned. "Well, I wouldn've said it like that, but you *can* stay if you want. Just don't expect miracles when you haven't extended mercy."

"Well, what does that mean?"

Lola laughed again. "It means if you stay, it's not an option to *not* forgive. Hell, if you leave it's not an option to not forgive."

Kendal remembered her dinner with Chase. He'd used the same exact phrase. Must've come from one of Mrs. Alexander's and her mother's chess night conversations. Those two old biddies and their late-life shenanigans might have been the very reason she was having a mid-life crisis now.

"You two ready to go? The church is only 15 minutes away, but I'd like to arrive at least 45 minutes early. I hope you're both prepared; we're going to be there the rest of the day."

"Yes, let me put my teacup away." Lola stood and went into the kitchen. Kendal stood and went to the bathroom. Kasey stood and shook her head. "Lord, help us all."

Kasey made her way down the busy city streets. For a Saturday afternoon, there was still enough traffic to be thankful for the extra drive time. Before resuming their earlier conversation, Kasey tried to read her sister.

"Kendal, you do know you don't need to explain yourself to anybody, right?"

"Absolutely not," Lola joined in. "You don't need to explain anything to everybody either."

"I know."

Lola turned around to look at Kendal. These should have been happier days, but Kendal's burdens had grown since the discovery of Jason's affair. She could give him her body, but no longer her heart.

Kendal sighed. "I asked God to break every soul tie, and He hasn't yet." Kendal paused. "I had to admit I'm still in love with Chase; I've always been. You're right, Mother. Chase has always been the one... even when I didn't want him to be."

"That's because the only reason you didn't want him to be was because he showed up an hour before you were marrying Jason," Lola laughed.

Kendal forced herself to look out the window while Kasey parked. "We're here," she announced. Kasey gathered her belongings and took notice of her sister. "Kendal, God hasn't broken your ties with Chase because you simply married Jason. A wedding doesn't give you a spiritual rite of passage."

"No indeed," Lola added. "You may be Jason's wife, but you're Chase's bride."

Kendal blinked and continued to stare into the distance. She heard and understood every word. Knowing just hadn't made it better.

"We all know you're hurting, Kendal. Just because you don't tell anyone, doesn't mean we don't know." Kasey closed her door and opened Kendal's. She took her sister's hand and helped her out of the back seat.

"Kendal, you expect people not to notice that you're not super woman," Kasey continued. "But, we all do. If no one else, Mother and I know you well enough to pay attention and take notice."

Kendal remained quiet. Lola spoke up. "Kendal, Honey, you missed your father's birthday."

Kendal raised her head. Lola kept talking. "You also missed Kasey's anniversary."

Kendal's eyes watered. "What? You guys..."

"Kendal, it's okay. We know..."

"No, it's not okay!" she shouted. "Oh, my God! What kind of daughter am I? What kind of sister am I?"

Kendal rested her body on the side of Kasey's car and closed the door. Since she'd been made aware of missing two very important dates, she'd also recalled declining every invitation she'd received in the last few months. Nobody had bothered to ask why, except Lola and Kasey.

Kendal cried. Kasey and Lola surrounded her with hugs. "It's okay, Kendal. We know you're not in a good place right now. It's okay to not be okay, sometimes."

"Yeah," Kendal sniffed. "But, what about everyone else?"

Kendal remembered several voice messages she'd received from girlfriends she hadn't taken time to call or schedule their monthly brunches with. She recalled the texts messages she'd received from people saying she never came to anything they had anymore, and her emotions got the best of her.

"Now, don't cry, Honey."

Kendal ignored her mother. Lola couldn't fix this one. There were people who didn't know about the affair, who hadn't heard about her in-laws, and who still expected her to carry the weight of their self-inflicted world upon her shoulders. She couldn't anymore. She was dying, and none of them had noticed.

"God knows your heart, Kendal," Lola reminded her.

"And, He also sees your character," Kasey added. "Don't let other people's insecurities become your own—not now, not ever."

Kendal wiped her eyes, before acknowledging Kasey had spoken. "I... I don't know what's wrong with me?" she admitted. "It seems all I do is cry. Not about the affair, not about the deaths, not even about the baby..."

Lola laughed, again. "I know this is serious, but girl it's obvious you're having an identity crisis."

Kendal heard her mother. She just wondered if the joke was on her. "I guess so. This is how smart people end up in stupid situations," she gathered. "Not to make excuses, but the politicians, entertainers, ministers, and CEO's... Me, Jason, Chase... This is how it happens."

"Well, not all of them," Lola urged.

"Absolutely not," Kendal affirmed. "But enough of them to lose their minds, their careers, and their credibility at the expense of their families. I can't let that happen. That's why I can't see Chase."

Kasey and Lola understood. "Well, you may not know who you are, but you haven't forgotten what you are not. I didn't raise hoes."

The three ladies laughed wholeheartedly in the parking lot outside of the church, then headed to the bathroom to fix their faces. "Oh, and one more thing," Lola added. "You both need to remember that some people would rather pretend they have a good marriage than tend to their marriage. You ignore all those voicemails and texts messages, Kendal. You're allowed to decline invitations. Work on you, Baby. Work on your marriage if you decide to. But, if people care enough to invite you and don't care enough to find out why you can't make it, especially if it's not like you to miss, then you didn't need to go."

"Mother, I couldn've said it better myself," Kasey concluded.

Chapter 18

"Stony, this is amazing! You really worked on this *all* weekend?"

"This—and this—alone," she admitted.

"Do you really believe Kendal and Chase could be happy?"

"I don't quite know yet, Liz? It's all unfolding as I go along. Maybe, I'll write a sequel. Why do you ask?"

"Just because; I was friends with someone for years. I loved him dearly, then one day he decided to take a chance on someone else."

Stony listened as Liz talked about a former friend who only dated Latin women. While he enjoyed her company and conversation, he never seriously considered dating her. Anything other than the occasional happy hour or weekend release of a new movie, and he hardly asked her out. Stony became curious and pried.

"Why did he only date Latin women? What was his ethnicity?"

"Well, he wasn't Latin if that's what you're asking."

"Oh, well, I thought maybe he was trying to stay true to his race."

"No, he said it was because Latin women are more open and giving."

Stony rolled her eyes. "Hell, there are five generations in one house. Yeah, they're open and giving. It's generational. Ain't no man ever left home. They support their families. They provide for their families. They don't leave their families."

Stony breathed and pulled herself back in. Had Liz been a client she never would've wrapped that in such a way. However, with her friend she knew she could be candid. Especially, if it helped Liz better understand it had less to do with her and more to do with him. "Sometimes, Liz, it just happens," Stony encouraged.

"For me, it just happens a lot."

Stony and Liz sat quietly. "I'm a good girl, Stony. Carmen... she is not." Liz let her voice trail. "My Chase married someone else. Now, Carmen has a man, and I don't."

Stony looked at Liz quizzically. She knew from the signs her *employee* was jealous but needed her *friend* to come to terms with and admit it for herself.

"First of all, Liz, Chase is not real. And, if he was, he would not have married someone else. Trust me. He would find you. Even if he did marry someone else; he would still find you. What's yours is just that... yours. Besides, is that why you give Carmen such a hard time?"

Liz didn't answer.

"Elizabeth, are you envious of Carmen and Luis?"

"I don't know. I guess so."

Liz really had no words. For far too long she'd watched Carmen go in and out of relationships. Sometimes, Carmen didn't even bother to mention her male friends because by the time they got around to meeting them, they would already be history.

"Listen to me, Elizabeth, don't you dare compare yourself to Carmen. Carmen is nothing like you, and you are nothing like Carmen. Let it go. Your prince will arrive one day and, when he does, he needs to find you. He isn't going to be looking for Carmen. And even if your friend stumbled upon her, even he wouldn't be looking for Carmen. He couldn't handle her. Carmen needed Luis."

Liz paused. "I know, Stony. It's just so hard sometimes. I mean, Carmen only cares about Carmen. How'd she end up with Luis? I mean, God must really have it in for me. Even Carmen has a man now. *Carmen has a man*," Elizabeth stressed. "God must really be running out of options up there."

“Liz, God doesn’t have it in for any of us, and He never runs out of options. It’s just not your season, yet. That’s all.”

“Well, I wish it would rain already. Because, this has been the driest spell anyone has ever had to go through.”

Elizabeth remembered her last relationship. She’d told several suitors since then she’d taken a vow of celibacy and like others before, they never spoke to her again. Without a trace, each would simply vanish like those before them.

“Stony?”

“Yes, Liz.”

“Sometimes, I do get lonely.” Elizabeth confided.

“I know, Liz. Sometimes, if I’m honest, so do I. Just remember, never give a person your body before you have their heart. If you sleep with someone before becoming friends with them, you have nothing to base the relationship on other than sex. Besides, God knows your struggle. He also knows your desires. Fight until you get what you want. That is, unless you want to end up like Sarah.”

“Sarah?”

Stony pushed the laptop aside and used finger drawings to illustrate what impatience looks like. With one hand she drew Abraham and Sarah, with the other she drew Hagar.

"Those are the worst stick-figures I've ever seen. My nephew draws better and he's four."

Stony ignored Elizabeth. Once she had Abraham and Sarah constructed, she completed Hagar holding a circle.

"What's that?"

"A baby."

"A baby? That's the ugliest-looking baby I've ever seen." Stony continued to ignore Liz, as she kept her focus. "Why is the woman with the baby in the middle?"

"Because, Sarah put her there," Stony stated matter-of-factly. "And, if you don't watch it, you might make the same mistake."

"That's a little far-fetched, Stony, don't you think?"

"No. It's not about the problem. It's about your position. You may never invite another woman to sleep with your man but, if you settle, he may just do it anyway. Patience, Elizabeth. Patience," Stony warned. "Opportunity will knock. Just be willing to wait for it."

"What are you two talking about?" Jessica entered and placed the box of chocolates from her weekend excursion in the middle of the table. "Where'd you guys go for dinner last night?"

"Nowhere," Liz volunteered. "I got dumped."

"What? By whom?"

"Stony traded me in for Kendal, Jason, and Chase."

Elizabeth sorted papers and listened to highlights of Jessica's weekend in Dallas. Since Richard had surprised her with a trip, that's all she had been talking about since their morning meeting. "The hotel was beautiful. The restaurant was spectacular," Elizabeth mimicked Jessica in her head.

"Okay, so tell us why you're glowing. It can't be a trip to Dallas alone."

"Amen to that, Stony," Elizabeth agreed.

"Girl, we slipped and slid for hours on a shower curtain!" Jessica exclaimed. She threw her hands in the air and patted her feet simultaneously.

Stony and Elizabeth looked at each other, as if neither heard Jessica's confession.

"Come again?" Elizabeth asked with a frown.

"I... did..."

Jessica emphasized her words and closed her eyes. When she shivered in her chair and opened her eyes, Stony and Elizabeth were staring her in the face.

"Uhm, please explain to the two non-sexuals in the room what you're talking about. I mean, I was married and still don't have a clue what you're saying, so I know Liz is thoroughly confused."

"Well, I've heard and seen some things in my life. "But, yeah, you lost me with that one, Jess. Yes, I'm confused."

"I don't know what got into Richard, but that man..." Jessica sat back and let another chill escape her body. Again, Stony and Liz stared her down. She could feel them looking at her before she opened her eyes, so she only opened one and closed it quickly. Jessica thought about Richard again, and a third chill went through her.

"That's it! What the hell did Richard do to you? Are you high? Stony inquired.

Jessica sat straight up with her ankles crossed. She couldn't stop what was going on. She didn't even know *what* was going on. Every time she thought about her husband, something happened. Her heart raced, her breathing intensified, her thighs throbbed, her butt squeezed together, and a chill started between her legs and shot upward until her shoulders arched, her neck jerked, her head rolled, and her eyes closed. If she kept this up, she would need new underwear before lunch.

"Jessica!"

“Oh, my God. Stony, I hear you. Girl, I’ve gotta go!”

“What happened?

“Girl, I don’t know. Richard...”

As soon as Jessica said his name, it started again. Jessica jumped up. “I... I have to go.”

Elizabeth looked at Stony. Together, the two grew more concerned. This was the first time Jessica had ever behaved in this manner. It was apparent something had gone wrong, and they intended to find out what.

Stony pulled out her phone to call Richard. When Jessica saw his picture on the LCD, she snatched the phone and ended the call. “I’m okay. Really, I am.”

Through heavy heaves, Jessica tried to convince Stony that it was nothing to be alarmed about. Besides, the last thing she needed was for Richard to know she talked about them with her friends in this much detail.

“What’s going on then?”

“Liz, girl, if you ever get a husband... baby oil and a shower curtain.” Jessica shook her head... baby oil and a shower curtain is all I’m saying.”

Elizabeth laughed and Stony raised a brow. “What! A shower curtain laced with baby oil? Who does that?”

Jessica sighed and fanned herself with her hand. "Before this weekend, I don't know. Since this weekend, Richard and I do."

Stony stood and shook her head. "So, you're over here feenin' for Richard? Lord, he's done turned you out…"

Elizabeth laughed at Stony. "Girl, if it's that serious, I'd better leave that baby oil and shower curtain where it is."

"I'm just saying," Jessica continued. She shook again. Elizabeth and Stony both burst into laughter. "You're just saying you need a battery-operated boyfriend right about now."

Jessica rolled her eyes and looked at her watch. She pressed one button on her phone after unlocking it and waited. "Hi, Honey, where are ya?"

Stony and Elizabeth cracked up. "This woman's making a midday sex call," Elizabeth whispered.

"Richard must've put it down. I've never seen Jessica like this," Stony added. "She needs vacations more often; don't know how to act."

"I don't think it was the vacation, Stony. I think it was the amusement park... all that slippin' and slidin'. Richard done finally turned her out."

"Okay, Honey, I'm leaving now."

Jessica hung up the phone. “My calendar is clear until three o’clock. I’ll be back then.”

Stony and Elizabeth watched in disbelief as Jessica exited the room sauntering out as she’d entered. Being part-owner had its perks.

Elizabeth recycled the empty boxes and Stony gathered her belongings as both shook their heads. Together, they exited as Martin entered.

“What’d I miss?”

Stony and Elizabeth both snickered. “Just more about Jessica’s trip,” Liz offered.

“She really enjoyed Dallas. Good for her. Any plans after work?”

“Yeah, she *really* enjoyed Dallas,” Stony concluded. “I’ll be writing. I’m always writing.”

“You, Liz?”

Liz looked at Stony, then back at Martin. Could opportunity be knocking? “Uh, no. Not really.”

Chapter 19

Stony closed her closet door and made her way to her home office. With Simba at her feet, she took her time clearing her mind as slowly as she had changed out of her suit. It was good catching up with her team. She hadn't been out of the house since leaving work the previous Friday, and now her weekend activities would resume. Consumed with the love triangle in her head, as soon as she was finished writing her story, she would be sure to take Carmen up on her offer for a night out... minus Luis' uncle.

Simba yipped to be picked up. Stony placed the pup in her lap and turned on the laptop that had become her only portal into Lala Land. Although everything wasn't quite perfect for Jason, Kendal and Chase, it was still perfect to her—the sheer expression of writing; the experience of seeing what they saw, smelling what they smelled, tasting and feeling as they tasted and felt... She'd become angry with Kendal and had cried with Jason. She'd hugged Lola and had slapped Simoné. Each character was a small part of her, yet she felt for them all individually as she had each of her patients.

Once logged in, Stony continued where she'd left off. Liz had enjoyed everything she'd read so far, and it was no small feat to hold her friend's attention. Jess was the reader; however, Liz had made the connection. Encouraged, Stony typed.

"Taking out his cell phone, Jason placed a call. "Hi, Sheldon. I need a few more personal days."

Truth be told, Jason had considered launching his own marketing firm for over a year. Although he had toyed with the idea several times, he hadn't been serious until ending things with Simoné. He'd accepted his fate once Kendal had found out but had earnestly tried to separate himself from his lover months prior.

With his parents' estate being settled, Jason tried to rebuild his life and family. He'd started researching the idea of entrepreneurship more frequently each day. Listening to the elevator music patiently before his colleague returned, he waited. "Okay, thanks for checking. I'll be in..."

"Listen man," Sheldon interrupted. "Take your time. You have enough days to last a few months. Just take your time."

"Thanks man, I appreciate it."

Everyone understood it would take time to regroup after losing both his parents. The insurance check had come and was more than enough to cover all of their burial expenses, final bills, and set him and his family up for generations. Because of his parents' generosity, Jason knew his grandchildren's grandchildren would have an inheritance long after he decided to invest his share into his own firm. If there would ever be a time to step out on his own, it was now.

The phone rang and broke his silence. Interrupting his train of thought, his brother-in-law was right on time for the conversation he'd promised himself he would have with Hayden.

"Hello."

"Is this a good time?"

"Sure. I've been expecting you."

Hayden was aware that Kendal was with Kasey and Lola for the weekend. He'd left them at the house earlier when Kasey was preparing for her women's event at another church. He could have called from home but didn't want to chance the ladies returning amid him and Jason's exchange.

"So, was there anything in particular you wanted to speak about?"

Hayden knew enough but still wasn't aware of everything. He hadn't prodded because, as a minister, he was fully aware that only those who admitted they needed help would receive it. So, he had waited for Jason or Kendal to come to him first. If neither did, he'd simply continue to pray that they sought the help they would eventually need—together or apart.

Jason cleared his throat and tried to swallow the lump that was forming. Other than with Kendal and David, he hadn't uttered Simoné's name. Ashamedly, he confided in Hayden.

"I've messed up and trying to keep it covered only made things worse."

"Go on," Hayden urged.

Unsure of how much Hayden knew or didn't know, courtesy of Kasey, Jason took a breath and exhaled. "Last year, I had an affair with a co-worker. Kendal found out just before Christmas and nothing's been the same since."

Hayden played devil's advocate. "Did you really expect it to be?"

"I really don't know what I expected," Jason admitted. "At least I know I never expected my parents to die at the hands of my ex-lover."

Hayden listened without judgment. "And, the baby?"

"I... I didn't know about the baby..." Jason's voice trailed. "I can only imagine Simoné was reaching out to me because of it."

Closing his eyes, Jason's words resonated in his head. For the first time he considered the child he lost and the one he had gained. According to the autopsy he'd paid the mortician for, Simoné was as far along as Kendal.

"I slept with Simoné one last time in Minnesota... before telling her I couldn't continue seeing her. That morning…"

Hayden put two and two together. "And, you came home and made love to Kendal when you returned?"

Jason's stomach now turned. He'd been the kind of man he had despised. The kind, apparently, his father... and his father before him... had been.

"Yes. That same night."

This time, it was Hayden's stomach that felt sick. Still, he found the words to speak. "Have you two spoken to anyone?"

"Like a counselor?"

"Yes! Exactly, like a counselor."

"No. David knows, but we haven't spoken to anyone together."

Hayden remembered meeting Jason's best friend and pastor on several occasions. Holiday parties and weekend get-togethers had been part of the Winters' life before the onset of the affair and it's impeding consequences.

"What advice did he give you?"

"He told me if I want to save my marriage, then I need to save my friendship."

"That's actually quite accurate," Hayden agreed.

"Yeah, but how do I do that when she constantly avoids me?"

Jason remembered happier times when he and Kendal had been inseparable. When he'd sit in his armchair, and she'd plop in his lap or be so close to him on the sofa, he'd be pinned. In the last few months, she'd distanced herself so much she was only coming when he was going.

Hayden detected a hint of hopelessness. From what he could gather, Kendal was simply trying to survive. She didn't have time for games or to play house; she was building, with or without him.

"When's the last time the two of you talked? I mean *really* talked."

Jason didn't take long to answer. "This morning before she left for Baton Rouge."

"Okay, so that's good. You're still communicating. How'd it go?"

"You tell me. I used the tactic you agreed with David on."

"Meaning?"

"Meaning, I told her I believe our friendship will sustain our relationship, as she was walking out of the bedroom towards the garage."

"Okay."

"Okay? She stopped and asked me if she was really my friend considering I'd lied, cheated, and withheld information."

"I see."

"Then, she told me we are not friends. We are partners. And, she left."

Jason remembered vividly Kendal's words on her way out the door. "We are not friends; we are partners. We have a house with a mortgage and four children together. According to an article I read online last week, children fair better after the age of seven in a divorce. I'm weighing my options."

Listening intently to Jason on the other end of the phone, Frank could no longer keep quiet. This time, he cleared his throat and stood to speak over Hayden's shoulder. "Son, it's my fault."

Stunned, Jason let Frank's words draw him out of his trance. A man of few words, he had no idea what his father-in-law was implying; he hadn't even known he was there.

"It's time to tell the truth. And, both of you need to hear this."

Frank moved closer to Hayden's office phone. "These are childhood scars. Kendal can't move past this because she's still being held hostage to her memories of me."

"You've been there the entire time?"

"Yeah, but it's no biggie. I was reading a newspaper. Hayden said he had a call to make, so I sat in a chair in the corner as always. I don't live here, so I don't know these people, and these people don't know me."

He had a valid point. Hayden had let his father-in-law sit across from him on several occasions while counseling a member of his congregation on the phone. The chances of Frank making any connections were as slim as turkey bacon.

Now that he was up, Frank looked at Hayden and spoke into the speakerphone. "Son, I learned the hard way you don't let your kids fight battles you could've won or put up with demons you could've conquered. If she comes home, love her. If she doesn't, love her. Either way it goes, she will never be the same."

Somehow, Jason knew Frank was right. Kendal hadn't been Kendal in months. Even though she came home every day, she didn't come home to *him* every day. Sometimes, she did; other times, she was merely a shell of her former self. It was his fault; he had done that to her. Now, her father was trying to shift the blame.

"Why would you say that?"

Frank filled Jason and Hayden in on the same information Kasey had been fighting herself to keep secret for 25 years. The only difference was he was able to speak first-hand.

"Let's just say, the last night I didn't come home, Lola died. The girls paid the price. I hadn't counted the costs... any of them. Kendal may not forgive you because her mom never taught them how to forgive me. I lost all three of my girls that morning when I did show up. I don't think Kasey has ever been hurt by any man but me. She smoked and drank so badly, she broke up with her boyfriend and never set foot in their house again to spare her mother. I'm sure she had her share of sex, but she never let it dictate love or a relationship. That's my fault; I own that."

Had Hayden not heard some of this already, he would've squirmed in his seat. Fortunately, Kasey had been able to open up to him like a book when they'd met. At the time, he was a bouncer in one of her favorite night clubs. She'd sit at the bar and drink herself into a stupor, and he would stay until she was ready to leave to ensure she got home safely, even when he'd been off the clock for hours. Neither of them knew then they'd be each other's saving grace, but their co-dependency on each other formed a bond that had yet to be broken. He had promised Kasey if she stopped getting wasted, he would start going to church. She had laughed at him and said she'd never set foot in another one. All these years later, he was a pastor, and she was a first lady.

Frank continued as Jason listened quietly, and Hayden waited patiently. "Kendal's been hurt enough for the both of 'em. Aside from me and you, I'm sure the only other person I know she loves is that boy from across the street... Chase... Chase Alexander—childhood sweethearts. Only bad thing is she probably still trusts him. It's a good thing they both travel so much. It's also a good thing they lost touch. Together, they would be like Superman and kryptonite."

To Hayden, Frank was now speaking gibberish. He'd understood him as it related to Kasey, but Kendal being somebody's kryptonite other than Jason was a foreign concept. However, to Jason, it all made sense.

Jason suddenly understood why Kendal loved basketball but wasn't partial to the players. "I know your type," she'd told him when they first met. "A new girl every three to four weeks," he recalled.

"Chase? Chase Alexander from the Dallas Mavericks?"

"Yep, that's the one," Frank answered his youngest son-in-law and let the words roll off his tongue like water.

"Wait a minute," Hayden interrupted. "You mean to tell me *the* Chase Alexander—franchise player of the soon-to-be National Championship team, *the Dallas Mavericks*, Chase Alexander?"

"Yeah, that one," Frank confirmed nonchalantly. "Now, let me finish. You two need to know when someone is afraid, they will either fight, take flight, or flee. Hayden, Kasey did all three. Jason, Kendal did neither. She froze. Now, she's thawing."

"Frank, I'm sure it's close to that but not that in particular," Hayden concluded. "It's fight, flee, or freeze."

"That's what I said. They will defend themselves, take off, or get stuck."

Hayden nodded, as he and Jason tried to grasp what Frank was saying. Kasey had never told him she knew the star player of an NBA team, nor had Kendal shared she'd loved anyone before Jason.

Frank continued, unaware that neither was listening. "Years later, we figured out both girls were stuck in that same night, reliving their own version of my nightmare. The pain was so great, they both shut down."

When Jason heard the words shut down, he came back again. "Wait. What did you just say?"

"I said, Kasey has dealt with her demons. But, Kendal is just now realizing she has them. You triggered something you didn't even know you could."

Frank's words hit their mark. Jason realized in that moment he was replaceable. He just hadn't known by whom. He wanted so badly to just tell her to get over it, so they could move on together but knew because he had been the one to wound her, it wasn't up to him to tell her how or when to heal.

As if reading his mind through the intercom, Frank concluded, "I used to tell their mom after all that, if she ended up pregnant, she'd cheated. She wasn't sleeping with me, so I knew just like I had my secrets, I had to accept she might go out and create her own."

Chapter 20

"If rings saved marriages, we'd have 'em on every finger," shouted an older petite woman from across the room.

Kasey wondered what she'd just walked into.

"And our toes," another stranger joined in.

"Excuse me," Kasey interrupted, as Lola and Kendal stood beside her. "I'm looking for Glenda Michaels. I'm the guest speaker."

"Dr. Nichols!" A third lady scrambled over to Kasey and her guests. "We're putting the finishing touches on everything. We didn't expect you to be so early."

"It's okay. I wanted to have time to settle in before I took the stage."

"Well, can we get you anything?" The strangers fussed over Kasey as if she was First Lady, USA.

"No, no. I'm fine. Mom? Kendal? Would either of you like anything?"

"Not at the moment," Lola informed. "Kendal, Honey, you okay?"

"I don't need anything but to know where the bathrooms are for when I need one. Otherwise, I'm fine."

The stranger smiled. "Well, it's good to have you all here. I'm Glenda, and I'll be your attendant for the event."

Kasey smiled. "Well, Glenda, thank you for your hospitality. I'm Kasey Nic..."

"I know who you are. We all know who you are," Glenda blushed. *"Dr. Kasey Nichols,"* she emphasized.

Kendal and Lola took in what they'd heard about first-hand. Lola beamed as she realized Kasey was the local equivalence of a celebrity now. She knew people came from across the country to hear her daughter speak this year, and she was overjoyed for her.

Glenda's two assistants finished putting away the remaining items. Their conversation had been interrupted by their Subject Matter Expert for the day, so the two scurried away to take their seats.

Last year, Kasey had created such a stir in the community with her no holds barred approach to couples' therapy for women only that people were still talking about it. She'd left them with a message so profound, women around the country were still talking about, posting, and tweeting #SleepLazarusSleep. The men thought they were all lunatics until one of them caught wind of its meaning and filled the others in. This year, with tons of opposition, the Lord had seen fit to send Kasey back despite the uproar she'd caused, and many participants had come with their own list of questions and topics to engage in during breakout sessions.

"Well, Glenda, this is my mother, Mrs. Lola Paige, and my sister, Dr. Kendal Paige Winters."

"Two doctors… You must be a proud mama," she said while shaking Lola's hand. "It's good to meet you both."

"Yes, I am," Lola beamed. "I'm fortunate to be the mother of a medical doctor and a religious one. One saves lives; the other saves souls… both equally important."

"I agree, and I'll show you all to the green room now," Glenda announced. "Then, we'll be ready to take the stage in about an hour or so."

Lola waited for Kendal to exit the bathroom before following Glenda to their seats. Kasey had already been seated on the pulpit, and Lola had refused to sit all the way up front. Acknowledging her mother and sister's presence, Kasey nodded and smiled when they sat to the left of the stage. She had no doubt it was her mother's idea.

"Good afternoon, ladies!" the hostess exclaimed from behind the microphone. "And, welcome to this year's "See You, Be True." Shouts and cheers erupted across the sanctuary, and the MC kept the excitement going. "This conference marks the beginning of a new you, a new me, and a new level of destiny!"

The ladies clapped and cheered some more. Lola and Kendal participated with the sea of women who had come out to hear Kasey speak. She'd done so many conferences in the last few months, it was becoming normal to hear about the women reacting to Kasey as their guest speaker. However, seeing it had an unusual effect. This was no typical conference, and there was nothing common or redundant about it. They'd just gotten started and the room was already on fire. Two songs had been sang, a few announcements had been made regarding silencing cell phones, saying hello to at least three people you don't know, etc.; but, the atmosphere had been set for a much bigger presence than Kasey would be able to bring on her own.

Walking to the podium once she had been introduced, Kasey spoke. "I'm grateful Mt. Harmony has invited me back to be your Women's Day speaker, and I am ready to pour into you what saith the Spirit of the Living God concerning thou." A few yeses and amens were heard above the praises. "After this song, the next voice you hear will be that of the Holy Ghost."

Kasey returned to her seat and prayed silently. The Praise and Worship team sang Casting Crowns' *Who Am*

I? and exited the stage as Kasey returned. Singing the chorus again, Kasey belted the lyrics she'd requested months earlier. A Casting Crowns fan, she enjoyed numerous artists but loved this song for its metaphors.

Reflecting on the verses with both arms raised, Kasey took a few moments to lift up the Lord. Had onlookers heard her and her family's conversation hours earlier, they may have had their doubts about the woman standing before them with her arms stretched and tears running down her face. What Kasey knew, that many hadn't discovered yet, is that Jesus loves us all—just as we are. When we stop trying to be who everyone else thinks we are or wants us to be, then we would truly be free.

Kasey had learned the hard way that if Christ hadn't cleaned her up from a life of drugs, alcohol, and sex, then cussing would be the least of her worries. Some things had fallen away swiftly; others, had lingered. If she had to choose then over now, cussing it was. But, she wasn't in this place for herself. She was interceding on behalf of her sister. If Kendal was ever going to break free, she was going to have to get out of her own way, and this was the first step. To surround her by others who were equally, if not more, dysfunctional would either open her eyes to the truth or close them for good. Kasey was willing to take a chance; Kendal was simply unaware.

As the song faded out, Kasey screamed in exaltation. Shivers went through her, and peace enveloped the crowd as the music played softly for moments on end. Finally breaking the silence, she dried her eyes and took several deep breaths. After praying and sharing her scriptural reference for the day, she proceeded.

"Are we ready to receive the blessing of the Lord?" Several people clapped and cheered some more. "Are *you* ready to receive *your* blessing from the Lord?"

With a resounding, "Yes!" the conference attendees stood and cheered. "Yes!" was heard sporadically from strangers throughout the sanctuary, as Kasey stood on the edge of the stage looking out into the crowd.

"Last year when I left," Kasey started, "many of you pulled me aside and asked numerous questions I had very little time to answer. I received thousands of emails, hundreds of phone calls, and dozens of letters. People were reaching out to me on Facebook, trying to find me on Instagram and Twitter, and asking me why I wasn't on every other social media platform I haven't named or even heard of. So many of you that my husband gave me an office at the church," Kasey laughed.

She hadn't lied. Before last year, she was fine working from home on her "side hustle" as she referred to it. Decorating a house here and there for friends made her happy and being there for Hayden gave her joy. The church phones were ringing nonstop for months after Kasey's message, so he told her she needed to be there to answer them and she had been since. Ministry had become full-time for her after that, and it was because Mt. Harmony took a chance on a no-name preacher's wife who simply loved the Lord, was honest about where she came from, and understood life was a process worth going through if you dared to understand yourself and your role in it.

"Because so many of you hungered for more of Lazarus, I decided that this year we would do things differently. In case you missed it last year, here's a quick recap and additional instructions will follow. Please turn your attention to the screens."

Kasey listened as the Media Ministry showed highlights of last year's conference. "What if you want Lazarus to sleep?" Kasey had asked. "Is it wrong to not want God to revive what is already dead? When you have already mourned the loss and grieved in pain over that thing that is dead in your life, is it okay to want God to just let it be?" "What if you don't want Lazarus raised? When is it okay to just let him sleep?"

The live audience shouted for joy with the one onscreen. "Is it okay to not want God to bring back what has already started to stink up your life? *Yes!"* Kasey had proclaimed a year ago in the very same place. "The sin was in doubting that Jesus could raise him from the dead; not in not wanting him to. In not believing He could; not in waiting to see if He would. Therefore, I ask you today, what is that thing you are praying God never wakes up? Get that thing in your mind and focus really hard. Now, tell it sleep Lazarus, sleep!"

The crowd went wild and the video faded into the distance. Shouts continued to pour in like a wave from one section to another. "Raise your voices," Kasey commanded, "and shout 'sleep Lazarus, sleep!'"

Chapter 21

Lola sat in astonishment. Kasey was almost as good as Hayden, if not better. It had been awhile since she'd attended one of her daughter's speaking engagements, and she'd noted that Kasey had come a long way from teaching Sunday School to being a keynote speaker.

As Lola beamed, Kendal listened. She hadn't considered anything in life she wanted to die. Even emotionally separated from Jason, she didn't wish him any ill-will.

Watching last year's highlights, Kendal wondered where she was and why she'd missed it. Although Kasey had given her a DVD, she hadn't sat to watch it but would be sure to do so as soon as she returned home and found it. Although it would be much easier if they continued to recap, she owed it to herself and Kasey to see and hear the first part of what appeared to be a life-changing experience.

Kendal blinked and saw Kasey heading in her direction. Glenda rushed to her side and gave her a bottle of water as the Event Coordinator directed the ladies with Kasey's instructions. "Remember, ladies, if you want to experience more of Lazarus, your breakout sessions will be held in the east wing. If you want pre-marital coaching, you're meeting in room 201. If you are single, saved, and satisfied go to room 117. If you are single, saved, and dissatisfied, join them." There was an eruption of laughter as the ladies exited the sanctuary. The MC continued, "If you are married and miserable, married and looking, or married and lonely go to 355. And, if you don't know where you are right now in this season, stay right where you are. Someone will come and find you." Again, laughter broke out. "When we're all done in our sessions, we'll eat and return to the sanctuary together. Otherwise, you are dismissed."

Women flooded the building in every direction. While there were many topics to choose from, Lola and Kendal supported Kasey and followed the others to the east wing. Apparently, this was a big enough deal to have gathered a panel of guest speakers, but Kasey had center stage. As thousands of ladies spread out in groups, the west wing of the worship center held those seeking personal development workshops, and the north and south wings housed those needing professional and financial development. Kasey would have only women interested in relationship development, and both Lola and Kendal were curious to see how this would play out.

Lola leaned closer to Kendal and whispered, "I hope they have married and looking separate from married and lonely when we get in this room. I'm not lonely, but I'm not turning my face away either. Look, Lola, look." Kendal laughed at her mother's attempt to be both funny and fresh.

"Well, I hope Kasey doesn't expect me to go at all. I'm not opening up to these people. I should stay in here with the ones who don't know where they are. That sounds just about right for me."

"No you're not either," Lola informed. "You're coming with me. I saw women of all nationalities, ages, shapes, and sizes head that way. I'm sure we can all stand to learn a thing or two from each other."

Lola and Kendal followed Glenda when she came back for them. Kasey was already instructing each group in the area of topics and key conversations. She would read their assignments and make her rounds, then report back to each group for a bit more personal attention.

Kendal and Lola took their seats beside the other ladies and waited. Like two new students on the first day of school, they clung to each other for comfort and familiarity. The two strangers who were in conversation when they'd first arrived sat across the table from them. Lola spoke first.

"Hello, I'm Lola. This is my daughter, Kendal."

"Hi," the younger of the two replied gracefully. "Pleased to meet you. My name is Jaiden with an 'i'."

"That's different but suits you well."

"Thank you, Lola. My mom thought I was a boy and refused to change it when I was born. She said she called my name when I was crying, and I stopped. So, I already knew who I was when I got here, and she wasn't going to mess me up."

The older of the two giggled. "I'd say you messed yourself up."

Jaiden rolled her eyes. "Nobody was talking to you, Rita. Why don't you introduce yourself? No, wait, I'll do it," she volunteered.

"Lola and Kendal, meet Margo Rita Jones."

Lola widened her eyes and Kendal covered her mouth. After a few moments, the two could not conceal their laughter. Embarrassed, Rita locked eyes with Jaiden and then lowered her head as the empty chairs near them were filled.

"Okay, ladies," Kasey announced upon arriving at the *Married Life* classroom. "I'm glad you all made it here in one piece. We had the largest group, so we had to combine several large rooms on every level."

"It could be worse," shouted an attendee. "We could all be in the budgeting class."

Kasey smiled, as the others laughed. She was sure she had the best and most lively groups. "Very true. Let's begin. We will read John 11:1-16 and begin our table discussions. When you have time, I would suggest you bookmark and read the entire passage of scripture. However, for the sake of time, the Singles are in the *Waiting it Out* workshop discussing John 11:1-16 (Die with Him), the engaged over in *Almost There* are discussing verses 17-37 (Keep this Man from Dying), and you ladies in Married Life will tackle verses 38-44 (Let Him Go). When it's all said and done, we'll resume in the sanctuary as a united group and encourage one another.

Oooh's and ahhh's filled the space. Even Kendal and Lola cringed unexpectedly. "Did she just say..."

"Hush, Mother."

Lola straightened up in her chair and sipped her bottled water. She and Kendal had always joked with Kasey about being renegade, but neither had any idea being a rebel had given her a national platform.

"Well, just so you know," Lola attempted to whisper, "I'm not sure if this is such a good idea. I mean what kind of minister opens up a discussion with let him go at a marriage workshop?"

"There isn't a kind." Kendal swallowed her own water. "It's just Kasey. That girl is going to get us run out of town."

"Well, not without a fight. Do you see how these women are acting like she's the Oprah Winfrey of the South?"

Kendal laughed. "You have a point."

"Okay, ladies, here we go," Kasey announced. Glenda assisted by passing out pastel-colored index cards.

Kasey smiled at Kendal and Lola again, then continued. "Each of you will receive one index card. Take out your writing utensils and on the first line write this statement, 'If you love someone set them free, and you might find out dot, dot, dot.'"

The ladies did as instructed. Kendal and Lola followed suit, and Kasey was relieved. She hadn't expected Kendal to willingly participate but was glad she was experiencing the conference for herself with their mother's assistance.

"Now, once you have that one phrase written down, I want each of you to complete it with only one additional sentence. For example, if you love someone set them free," she began, "and you might find out they don't want to go anywhere. Get the idea?"

Again, the ladies laughed. "Or, better yet," Rita suggested, "how about if you love someone set them free, and you might find out you're better off without them?"

Kasey chuckled, as the remaining ladies howled in laughter. "You get the idea."

"Amen," several women chimed in. "Amen."

"I've got one," another attendee shouted. "If you love someone, tell them you want to see other people. You might find out they do, too."

Not a dry eye or closed mouth remained. The women all burst into laughter, simultaneously wiping their eyes. Regaining control of the room, Kasey reeled them back in after several moments to get herself together again.

"Looks like you should be going back to the Singles squad with me," Kasey joked. Laughter began again before the ladies settled down. "You ladies get started on your index cards. I'll be back as soon as I'm finished addressing the pre-marital group. This is why I chose to break you all up first. *Almost There* is not ready for you all yet."

"If they had any sense, they'd be *Waiting Forever,"* another stranger rattled off. Kasey concluded that mixing a group of married women together, who ranged from newly married to never should've married, might not have been such a great idea. With only the more seasoned ladies speaking up, she wondered if any newlyweds would engage in the conversation.

Focusing on her task when she returned, Kasey continued. "Fill out your index cards and discuss amongst yourselves what each person wrote in your group. You're gonna need the other side later. You may want to hold onto your seats, too. It's gonna be a bumpy ride."

Chapter 22

"I'm wrapping up now. Be out in a few."

Stony returned the phone to its carrier. Her sessions with Fletcher and Faith had gone especially well. Unsure of which route Faith would take, they'd both made their own separate progress. Although she hadn't seen them, Fletcher still held onto Faith, and Faith tried to regain hope that things could be better.

Making her way into the lobby, Stony acknowledged Liz and greeted her clients. The couple followed behind her at their own pace.

"So, what brings you in today? Together?"

Fletcher cleared his throat and spoke up. "Faith has been diagnosed with stage four breast cancer."

Stunned, Stony waited as if he would repeat himself automatically. After a few seconds of silence, she spoke up. "What did you just say?"

"I have stage four cancer."

Stony covered her mouth, as her eyes widened. "But how? When?"

"It's a long story, Dr. Rhodes. We're glad you had time to see us on such short notice."

Fletcher had called Stony at Faith's request when they left her physician's office. It had been a short ride but a long trip.

As Stony gathered her thoughts, Faith reached for the Kleenex on the table. "I was diagnosed several months ago."

Stony thought back to their last few visits. She remembered telling Fletcher she was there to save the two of them; saving the marriage was optional. She replayed earlier conversations with the couple about placing more value on time than things, kids included. Separate the children were simply little people; however, together they were an item... a thing. And, *anything* you put before your mate was bound to cause problems. If there was one lesson she could teach them and hope they had considered, it was protecting their time together and scheduling their time apart.

"Faith... Fletcher... I'm so sorry," Stony started.

"Don't, Dr. Rhodes," Faith interrupted.

"It's okay. I've already made my peace with it."

"But, in the last session, you didn't say anything."

"There was no need to. We were trying to decide what our next step was. I mean, at this point, our marriage is the last thing I'm thinking about."

"Faith..."

"It's okay, Dr. Rhodes," Fletcher interrupted. "We've made our peace with it together."

"I'm not sure what that means," Stony confessed.

"It means, I'm not having chemo."

"What? Why not? I mean, I'm sure there are some options you haven't considered yet."

"That's what I said," Fletcher admitted. "But, she's made up her mind.

"Excuse me." Stony picked up the phone. "Yes. Okay. Sure, I'll be there."

Still in disbelief, she couldn't figure this one out. Hanging up the phone, there were many more questions she wanted to ask, but respected the couple's privacy. Standing up, she didn't hide her disappointment.

"Is there anything you need?"

Fletcher looked up and Faith answered. "Yes, I want you to perform my eulogy."

"What?"

Fletcher lowered his head again. This was a conversation they'd had for weeks on end. "Faith, I'm not sure I understand."

"Sure, you do. It's Faith... the faithless."

"I hope you didn't intend that to be funny."

"Dr. Rhodes, I'm not laughing. She's serious. She doesn't want chemo. She doesn't want help. She just wants to go peacefully, and she wants you to deliver her eulogy."

"But, why?" Stony looked at Faith somberly. It was hard to remain professional after receiving the news of Faith's cancer and the request for a funeral in the same day. "Why won't you fight?"

Fletcher stood. Every question Stony had asked, he had beat her to. Faith had yet to answer. "Agree to do my eulogy, and I'll let you know."

"I... I need more time."

"Dr. Rhodes, time is one thing I don't have. I'm going to die. I'm asking you to speak on my behalf... to be my voice."

Lost and confused, Stony agreed to help Faith any way she could. "Faith, I have to tell you this is not what I had in mind, but I'm here for you."

"Good. It's settled. I'll send you everything you'll need, including my answer. My fight is over. I'm preparing to live."

Fletcher shook his head. Stony wiped her eyes. Faith smiled. "I know this isn't what you had in mind when you said you could help us get anywhere we wanted to go, Dr.

Rhodes, but thank you. Thank you for being here for both of us. Fletcher will be setting up appointments for the children in the coming weeks. We no longer need to come."

Stony understood. Faith had already decided what was in her own best interests. This was when she would rather be spending time with Kendal and Chase. When time had run out, she asked herself what would matter most... Jason being happy, or Kendal being free.

In this moment, Faith was helping her more than she had managed to help Faith. Where two worlds collided before her eyes, and four hearts broke under the weight of the world, Stony stood in this moment silently defeated and selfishly victorious. Fletcher and Faith were real; they were pale in comparison to Kendal and Chase. Still, they mattered equally as much.

So many of her characters had made their way onto the pages of the book with the characteristics of her clients, it was hard to draw a line. Where Jason and Fletcher were blurred, Kendal and Faith had merged. Two were living; the other two were dying. Asking herself one last question, she turned to Faith. "If you could change one thing, what would it be?"

Faith smiled once more. "It'll be included with the other information."

"Dr. Rhodes, my kids are having a hard time coping. One plays basketball, the other baseball. Maybe you could find a way to tie it all in to one big game. You know, my final score."

Stony stopped. In all her years of counseling, she hadn't lost a patient to death. She'd lost some to divorce, others to greed, but not one had died. She knew what Fletcher was dealing with. Although Malcolm never denied treatment, the time had finally come when it no longer benefitted him.

"I'm sure I'll be able to come up with something, Faith. You take care of you. I'll take care of your request."

For the first time, Faith hugged Stony, and Fletcher shrugged. "Guess I'll be seeing you around."

"Yes. I'll keep the books open for your call."

Stony took a minute to gather her thoughts when the door closed. Today, she couldn't walk them to the lobby. She couldn't walk to the bathroom to fix her face or freshen up to meet her girls either."

"Liz, something came up. Tell Jess I'll drive myself."

"Are you sure? We can wait."

"No, no. I'll be okay. I just need a little more time to myself. You guys can start without me."

Stony hung up the phone and stared at the sonogram picture on the wall and the pictures of she and Malcolm on her desk. She'd lost her husband and her child. Her father had been gone some years before, and had it not been for her mom, Carmen, Liz, and Jess she would have no family. These were the times when she wondered why life was so unfair. Faith had walked though her door a healthy, although unhappy, middle-aged married mother of two. Today, she walked out the same door unhealthy, seemingly at peace, not concerned about her marriage, but focused on her children.

"Oh, Faith..."

Stony cried. There was no way she could celebrate with her girls tonight, but it had been just as long since she'd seen them all together as it had been since she'd seen Fletcher and Faith in one session.

Clearing her mind, she turned out the light and stopped in the bathroom. She would go, but she would not rejoice. After a few moments, she was ready to walk out.

"Martin, I didn't think anyone was left."

"Yeah, I had to come back for something. You okay?"

"Yeah, just received some unexpected news from an unlikely person."

Martin could tell something had upset his colleague and friend.

"You sure? I can hang out awhile longer."

Stony propped herself up on the wall and let her weight shift. Martin reached out his hand and took hers. Although her makeup was intact, her eyes were red. The more she'd thought about Faith in the restroom, the harder she'd cried.

"Anything I can do?" he offered. "I know some people."

When Stony didn't respond, Martin apologized. "I'm sorry. That was supposed to be a joke."

"I know. Not very much is funny right now."

Martin led Stony to the lobby and offered her a seat. "So, what has you this upset? I saw the Whittington's leave. Anything to do with them?"

Stony considered her words. She could never breach her clients' confidentiality. "I just found out someone has cancer and is denying treatment."

The more Stony thought about it, she remembered it was stage four. Typically, by that time the treatments wouldn't work but still she would've preferred Faith try. Stony sat a few moments longer in silence with Martin.

She knew there was little he could say and didn't expect much.

"Well, you think you're gonna manage?"

"Yeah, I have to. I was asked to give the eulogy."

"Wow. That's different."

"I know."

Stony sat a little longer. Just as she was preparing to get up, her phone buzzed. Checking the messages, she sent a reply and stood.

"Thanks, Martin. I've got to get going."

"No problem. Anytime."

Stony gathered her rolling bag and purse. "So, how'd things go with Liz the other night?"

"Actually," Martin smiled, "better than I thought it would. She's quite a woman."

"That, she is. She has a good heart, and her head is on tight."

"I agree. Absolutely."

Martin escorted Stony to her SUV. "Drive safely. Call if you need anything."

"I will." Stony drove the few blocks to their usual spot. The trio was seated and waiting. "What did I miss?

“Late. Late. Late,” Carmen announced. “Always late.”

When Stony didn’t return a joke, Carmen raised a brow. “Are you okay?”

“Yeah, just got some bad news, but we’re not here to talk about that.”

“Stony, you know we can talk right?”

“Yeah, so fill me in. What are you and Luis up to these days?”

“Finally,” Jess jumped in. “She wasn’t going to tell us until you got here.”

“Well, spill it.”

Carmen sipped her margarita before speaking. “He wants to marry me.”

Chapter 23

Stony struggled inside. Although it was quite warm, even for March, she was indescribably cold. She'd mourned with Faith and had celebrated with Carmen. Still, she had to concede it hadn't been the best day. Faith's news overshadowed Carmen's, by far.

Setting the alarm to stay, she left her bags at the door. The walk into her office after a night out with her girls had typically been full of mental notes that randomly filled her pages in one chapter or another; however, tonight was different. There were as few thoughts of Kendal as there were of Chase. Jason was non-existent at the time. In the moment Faith had communicated that she'd accepted she was dying, all creativity flowed to and settled on Kendal. Kendal... the one who had loved and lost... the one who had given and not quite yet received a return on all she was worth.

Stony dried her tears and sat at her desk. She'd tried to keep her clients and characters separate for months. While general in the broad context of life, none were readily identifiable to all; yet, each was very recognizable to her. She'd worked with the Whittington's and had hoped they would survive. Even if she'd never share her personal desires in a professional setting, she'd cheered for dozens of the couples she'd counseled. Faith and Fletcher were no different. The truth was more had split than had been sustained. While their umbrellas were out, not many were able to actually weather the storm. Once the train pulled out of the station, each party was on their own journey. Some returned together; others didn't return at all.

As she powered her laptop on, Stony considered Faith. Then, as she logged in she considered Kendal. She couldn't tell where the lines had been crossed. She just knew something had transpired between her last chapter and the next one.

Blowing her nose, Stony exhaled. Her heart broke for Faith just as it had for Kendal. Death was death. She'd counseled plenty of women through their husband's infidelities but had never counseled one who had chosen to look Death in the face and smile. For Faith, Death had been a welcomed visitor. For Kendal, it had become an unexpected friend. The how's and why's had trumped Fletcher and silenced Jason.

Stony literally had no words. Staring at the LCD screen, thoughts of Chase came to mind. Reminiscent of Life, he was Kendal's connection to the sun. The energy that flowed between them gave her all she needed to go on. Faith had turned her children into her joy. Not sure how long she had left, she'd vowed to hold onto them until they had to let her go.

Kendal, on the other hand, had relinquished all hope of having joy again. She'd held her children longer and had squeezed them tighter, but they couldn't get any closer. Even the one growing inside of her wasn't privy to all of her. Jason had made sure of that when he'd given parts of her to another woman.

Stony sighed. Tonight, for the first time, there would be no writing. No heart-felt advice from Kasey, no laughs from Lola, nothing. She was empty. Maybe that's the way it needed to be. Tonight, she needed to let reality simmer. Faith was dying. Fletcher would be a widower. Although neither had said anything, she knew they would be fine. Their marriage was no longer an issue when you sat it next to Faith's diagnosis of cancer. Divorce or death was a tough choice. Even if Faith chose the latter, Fletcher would have to live with the prior. Their marriage had ended before Stony had ever met them. Now, their lives were beginning since they'd left her. Somewhere, she'd hoped to be able to bridge the gap. Given enough time, she was sure they would've made it. But, neither of them would ever know now.

As if getting a second wind, Stony turned to face the monitor again. When she'd left off, Kasey was in the midst of a women's conference with Lola and Kendal in attendance. While she had been confident of every scene and every character's role in it, things had significantly changed within the last few hours. Completely unsure of what she was supposed to do with the pieces she currently held, Stony typed her way through puffy eyes.

"All the single ladies!" Kasey announced over the P.A. system. When the microphone echoed, the ladies all stopped and stared. "Thank you for attending this year's *Waiting it Out* workshop." Applause went through the room. "Now, regarding your Bible verses, I will read 1-15 and we will read together, aloud, John 11:16. The ladies all stood as Kasey read and, on queue, joined her in reading the last verse.

"Sixteen," they chimed in, "therefore Thomas, who is called Didymus, said to his fellow disciples, "Let us also go, so that we may die with Him."

"Amen," Kasey concluded.

"Amen," they responded.

Listening to Kasey summarize the passage of scripture, the ladies took notes as she explained what was familiar to some and foreign to others. "From the verses, we can conclude that one man is dead already, Lazarus. Now," Kasey went on, "we also know that man has two sisters, Mary and Martha." The ladies listened attentively to Kasey as she spoke clearly and remained upbeat. It was as much what she was saying as it was how she was saying it.

"Mary and Martha, together, sent word to Jesus letting him know Lazarus, your boy, is sick." A few snickers broke out. "It's there," Kasey reassured. "Jesus loved Lazarus and his sisters. They were like all the people in our lives who aren't really kin to us that we call our play sisters and play brothers, or even our play cousins." Kasey knew, because growing up all she had was Kendal and Chase for the most part. Chase was her real brother, let her tell it, but her school buddies were really in the play category.

"So, when Jesus found out, his response was 'this sickness is not to end in death, but for the glory of God.' Then, the Bible reiterates that Jesus loved Martha, and her sister and Lazarus. See?" Several people nodded in agreement and others said, "Amen," again.

"Now, even knowing Lazarus—his boy—was sick, Jesus tarried. In fact," Kasey went on, "he waited two days. Say it with me, *"Two days."* The ladies did as instructed. *"Two days."*

When Kasey picked up at the next verse, she brought it all together for them. "Jesus said to the disciples two days later, let's go. Now, seriously, how many people can you actually think of that you honestly love and would let wait two days for you to decide to even go and see them when you heard they were sick?"

A few "wellllls" entered the air along with some additional laughter.

"Oh, I get it," Kasey agreed. "But, well, now think about if the shoe were on the other foot? I mean, wouldn't you wonder what took so long?"

The ladies laughed again but kept up with Kasey. "Look at it. It's all there in the verses. You see it?"

"Yeah, it's there."

"Yes, it is."

"Uhmn humn."

Kasey surveyed the room. Of those who responded, she was fully aware they were paying attention. Those who had not, she knew they were listening attentively. Either way it went, Bible is Bible. As long as she stayed true to the Word of God, it would do what it was intended to do. Her part was easy; tell the story. The rest was up to the Holy Ghost to revise and edit. It wasn't her story; it was the Lord's.

Kasey watched as more ladies pulled out pens and joined those already taking notes. She gave them additional time before proceeding. "Let me tell you something, ladies. The season you are in is always the best season to be in—even seasons of waiting. The only alternative is death. You're either here and waiting, or you're not here and not waiting. The simple fact that you're alive is praiseworthy."

Claps rang in the air. From simply alone to miserably lonely, they were all single. Once married and now divorced, never ever engaged, or possibly widowed and somewhere in between, today their common ground was their saving grace... they were all waiting it out.

"Today, we discover how to accept where we are so that when we cry, we know when it's best to let the tears fall or head for the hills. We will get past the 'bad boys ain't no good, good boys ain't no fun' phase. This is life, ladies, and it's coming for each of you. Are you ready to die with Him?"

Chapter 24

Chase sat in the corner nursing his cranberry juice and watching the crowd. With their latest victory under his belt, the Dallas Mavericks were now headed into the finals. He hadn't heard from Kendal since they'd last met over dinner and not being able to celebrate with her was finally weighing him down. This was one of the biggest nights of his career, and the players had spared no expense. Without her to share it with, being there was pointless.

"Man, you're missing out."

Chase looked up at his teammate who was busy nodding and smiling in the direction of every pretty face he saw.

"You still thinking about that doctor you ran into back in Chicago? Man, I keep telling you... you can't covet somebody else's wife and think it's okay."

"She's not his wife," Chase scoffed.

"Uh, the county clerk would beg to differ."

Chase remained silent. He knew that although Kendal had married Jason, she hadn't become his wife. Titles came in many shapes and forms, and being married didn't make you somebody's husband or wife any more than sitting in a garage made you a car.

"Listen man, have you slept with her?"

"What? No," Chase retorted with a frown and a heavy sigh.

"Well," shrugged his teammate, "I tried to help you out."

"Help me out? By asking me if I've slept with her? What kind of help is that?"

"Well, if y'all would pay attention, you would remember when I said everybody you sleep with in the natural, you marry in the spirt. I was trying to help you out, but she ain't even your wife physically. He married and wed her before you ever held her."

"Is that supposed to be funny?"

"Actually, yeah. I'm used to seeing you posted up with two or three honeys. You over here holding onto a glass of juice like it's the sweetest thing in the room."

Chase took in the words his comrade had spoken. He remembered their conversation about Kendal when he'd gotten back from Chicago. When he'd made it back to the airport, a few of them were sitting around talking about all the women they'd met in the few days they were there.

Some had merely met, others had consummated relationships they weren't even in.

"Yeah, I remember." Chase surprised his teammate.

"What?"

"I said, I remember your words about not sleeping with anybody you don't want to wake up married to."

"Ah, so you were listening?"

"Oddly enough, yes. And, I haven't been with anyone since before Chicago."

"What! *You?*"

Chase raised his glass and took the final sip of his drink. He had only spoken of Kendal as an old childhood friend who was now a doctor in town on a medical emergency as they were leaving Chicago. He'd been asked if she was married, and he'd answered. Other than that, no specifics... no details. Afterwards, he'd only gone into depth with his mother and Kasey.

"This one's for you and your friend."

Chase released his thoughts and raised his empty glass next to the other player's.

"Say, man, you want another glass of juice?" he joked.

"No, I'm good. Besides, it's not cool that you get on the players for sleeping around then you drink up."

"Did you just call me a hypocrite?"

"If the jock fits..."

"Ah, a'ight. I hear ya. That's cool. You just be on the lookout."

"Lookout? What for?"

Chase followed his friend's eyes and noticed his newest admirer. "Nah, I'll pass."

"You serious?"

"Yeah, I told you I haven't been with anybody."

"Yeah, but you didn't say you wouldn't."

"Man, you're a joke." Chase shook his head. "You just talked about not sleeping with anybody you don't want to wake up married to, and you're surprised I actually listened."

"Hey, I just wanna be sure all of you understand there will be consequences and repercussions on Judgement Day. As your boy, I need to be sure you understand you can't be sleeping around and depositing pieces of yourself into other people and expect to get married and be whole. Why do you think the divorce rate is so high?"

"Because people realize they messed up."

"No, because people realize they either didn't have anything left to give the one they married, or they never wanted to give 'em anything in the first place."

Chase stared in disbelief. *This dude is actually making sense and giving me something to think about.* He knew Kendal was the latter; he would be the first, which is why he had remained single. He had decided long ago that marriage would be on hold because he had always figured he had nothing to give that anybody really wanted. Sure, he could provide for a family. But, he had always been guarded. His parents and life had taught him well. Anyone who couldn't tell you why they loved you beyond the natural didn't really love you. In his life, there had been many women who wanted his offerings but very few who had wanted him. High school had set the stage. When it was all said and done, all the popular girls wanted a baller. Kendal simply wanted him.

Chase never had a problem giving of his time or sharing his resources; he just made sure everyone knew he was no fool upfront. If he spent money, it was because he wanted to and not because he was expected to. If you stayed over, it was because you were invited; not because you decided. He hadn't been able to say 'I love you' to not one woman in all those years, still many who would settle for his bank account lingered.

"Okay, either you're sick, or this woman is packing platinum."

Chase refocused his attention and responded to the sound of the other player's voice after a few moments. "What'd you say?"

"I said give me the good doctor's number, so I can see for myself."

"Slow your role, player. Kendal is off limit for jokes."

"Kendal. Humn. Off limits... Humn. You're serious."

"Yes, I am. All jokes are off on that one. Besides, you can have that one over there. She's okay."

"Okay? She's the finest one in here tonight."

"Yeah, she's Dallas cute though. Kendal is international cute."

Chase got up and headed for the exit without another word. He heard his name being called but refused to turn around or answer. Nothing he wanted was there, and everything he needed was home.

"Leaving?"

Chase stopped and smiled at the mysterious woman who had followed him through the hotel lobby. As he waited for the valet driver to return with his car, he wished Kendal would appear.

"Yes, I am."

"Would you like some company?"

Trying to remain cordial, Chase politely declined when his car was parked. A few months sooner all bets would be off. He would never have even left the hotel; he would've had a room. She wouldn've had to ask; he would've given her a key.

Chase sped out of the driveway headed for his estate. *That was a first.* He considered that he'd never turned a woman down. Well, not a fine one. Since reconnecting with Kendal though, no one else compared. He could make love to her breathing in the silence they'd shared on earlier phone calls or blow off some steam with a gold-digging stranger who'd be okay with a few drinks tonight and a new outfit tomorrow. He'd done that more times than he cared to admit, so bailing now wasn't a bad time to start a new routine.

The privacy gate opened, and Chase slowed his car to turn inside. Resting his elbow on the door, he rubbed his brow and closed his eyes when he parked. *I miss her.*

Chase recognized the familiar feeling he'd had for years. With no way to describe what it was or how it made him feel before Chicago, he'd blown it off and covered it with the strangers he'd often woke up next to. Now, he knew without a doubt the feelings he'd masked for decades were remnants of his non-relationship relationship with his childhood best friend. He'd missed her and hadn't known it until he'd seen her again. Now, having not seen her, he was fully aware what that level of loneliness felt like. No amount of money and no caliber of sex would make it better. What he wanted was his friend; what he needed was her.

Chase entered through the washroom and removed his clothing. Making his way upstairs, he considered his mother. If it wasn't for her telling him to put himself in her husband's shoes, he would be undressing the love of his life right now, instead of walking up the staircase naked and alone. Coming home with Kendal would have been rewarding enough to have missed the entire party. Even if they only held each other in the quiet of the moonlight, having her close enough to touch her would be more beneficial than being miles away and only able to feel her.

At the top of the stairs, for the first time, Chase realized how much unnecessary space he had. As he climbed into bed, the only thing on his mind was Kendal. He had carried her in his heart for decades. There was something about the way she talked to him. Something in the way she touched him and held him. There was something in the way she laughed and smiled... in the way she walked and smelled. She just was.

At the end of every night and the beginning of each new day, it was always Kendal. The woman he wanted, the woman he needed, the woman he loved. For her, he would give it all up. For Kendal, he would. He'd wasted enough seed on meaningless sex. The next time he was with someone, he would be making love to her.

Chase had fallen asleep with Kendal and hadn't touched her. Next time, he would wake her. He would marry her, then he would wed her. Both Kasey and his mother would simply have to understand. He would wait it out. But, when she called for him, he would be ready. His life was full of competition and, married or not, Jason wasn't going to stop what had already begun. He was already running out of time; however, Chase was just getting started. He'd given her room to breathe, and he would gladly hold his breath on her behalf.

Chapter 25

"Love, when left to the imagination, can be your best friend or worst nightmare. Don't wake up and find out you're in the wrong season with the right one, or the right season with the wrong one."

Kasey wrapped up her introduction with the ladies in the pre-martial session. "Now, since we've got that out of the way, turn with me to John 11:17-37, and let's take a look at what the text has to say about it."

Kasey waited as each person either opened their bibles or their apps. "I want to be clear about who my audience is; therefore, let us begin." She opened her Bible and rendered further instruction. "I will read verses 17 through 36. Please join me when we reach verse 37. Amen?"

"Amen," the group responded in unison.

"I must tell you, the ladies in *Waiting it Out* are fired up. Those Singles are up for the challenge. When this is over, we will attempt to pair each of you who are *Almost There* with one single and one married woman. Your task is to pour into the one "waiting it out" and glean from the one "enduring married life." This isn't a class you take and leave; this is a lesson you live out and apply. Once you *get there*," Kasey emphasized, "*Married Life* begins."

Claps rang in the air, and Kasey proceeded, "Stand with me, if you will, for the reading of the Lord's Word." Beginning at verse 17, Kasey read fluently as she had before. "And, now, altogether at verse 37... But some of them said, "Could not this man, who opened the eyes of the blind man, have kept this man from dying?""

The ladies took their seats and waited. Kasey knew from watching them they weren't going to be as fired up as the Singles or as radical as *Married Life*. They were happy to be getting married and had come for a "how to" or "what not to" on or in marriage. They would soon discover this was going to be more of a "speak now or forever hold your peace" rally. If she did this right, half of them would post-pone or cancel their weddings, regardless of the money they'd spent. Saving yourself was worth losing the money. If she did not, she'd hear about it a few years from now when they found her after losing themselves or their men.

The ladies sat quietly, as if awaiting a classroom lecture. They knew, by now, the Singles were deep in conversation surrounding whatever activity Kasey had challenged them with. Several of them were in the Singles workshop this same time last year, so they would be double blessed by Kasey's revelations from building on last year's message. Although she hadn't divided them into groups, her introduction to *The Lazarus Effect* had resonated to the degree that it now required multiple stages at the same conference.

As Kasey followed the success of her previous format, she walked the ladies through a summary of each verse. "I want to focus on verse 37; however, to give you all an idea of the backstory, let's start where *Waiting it Out left off.*"

Kasey worked highlights of the Single's lesson into the second part of her intro. As she explained where Jesus and his disciples were, she pointed out that this narrative had less to do with Lazarus, and more to do with Mary and Martha. For the Singles, it was Jesus and the 12.

"For starters, how many of you ladies have at least 12 good friends?" Kasey raised her hand and waited. Only a small percent of the room joined her.

"Wait, am I in the right place? You're all getting married, and you don't have at least 12 bridesmaids?" Laughter erupted, as expected. "Okay, well, I just wanted to point out that if your entourage is bigger than Jesus', then you really are in the right place. "Keep this Man from Dying" has your name written all over it because you have the manpower, excuse me," Kasey corrected herself, "the *woman*power... *girl* power... *she-man*power to raise the dead."

"Come on, now!" someone shouted.

"Yes, girl! Go on with yo' bad self!" another added.

Kasey smiled. In her flesh, she would've soaked it all up and made it about her, but her task was bigger than herself, and it brought her no joy to be the bearer of bad news. Yes, there was the Good News of the Gospel, but there was also a valley at the bottom of every mountaintop.

Kasey went on as the ladies quieted themselves again. "As I was saying, each of you will have the power to raise the dead and, truth be told, you're gonna need it." There were no cheers and no applause.

Kasey continued to fill in the blanks regarding the scripture verses and brought the women up to speed. Glad Kendal wasn't in this session, she kept going. "Sometimes, the Lord will call you out of your house to deal with what's dead and gone in your lives. Any bodies anyone need help getting rid of?"

Laughter returned, and Kasey quickly heard pages turning around the room. Like the Singles group before them, something had stuck. Giving the ladies time to capture the note, she rephrased it.

"There will be times when you will be required to get up, get moving, and get out. You need to know that going in. Everything ain't always built to last. I know. I know. Sorry to break it to you, but the reality is, the odds are not in everyone's favor."

"What did she just say?" echoed throughout the room.

"I said, you get to be Jesus. This man you say you love enough to marry, do you really love him enough to keep him from dying?" Kasey thought of her brother-in-law. Jason was certainly on the brink of death and was clueless about it.

Kasey laid out the pre-marital activity for the day. "Over the years, I have wondered why let Lazarus die and let so many people be pained by it, when all Jesus had to do was show up. And, ladies, another moment of truth for you: some of you are going to have moments when you wonder why God won't just do something. Why He won't just fix things."

Kasey could sense the discomfort and held her breath for a while. She wanted this one to sink in more than the others. "Jesus loves each of us, but He will not spare any of us where His glory will be revealed. If He has to let something die in your life, He will let something die in you first. And, most often, you will have to be the one who gets to roll the stone away."

"Ouch!" permeated the room.

"I know. I know. That's not comfortable, but neither is marriage 100% of the time. So, if you're looking for a timepiece, you need to exit now. This workshop is for wives. And, let me tell you, you've got to be born ready to be a wife. You can't just get ready and be a wife. No amount of makeup, no amount of hair, not even the most beautiful wedding dress, nor the most expensive ring can help you. You need to decide right now if you're here to play dress up, or if you're here to put up. Because marriage, good or bad, is always going to cost you something. If you weren't born ready, you will never *be* ready."

A gasp as loud as the earlier laughter was heard. "Let me just plug this in here." Kasey felt the boldness of the Holy Spirit come upon her and kept right on. "Sometimes, love is a beautiful dream. Other times, it's nothing more than a beautiful nightmare. Turn to your neighbor and tell them, 'Don't fall for the illusion'." Now, turn to the other side and say, "Don't *be* the illusion."

Some of the ladies did as asked; others continued to take notes. Kasey waited for all.

"Most women just want to be able to say they have a man… Somebody to go to dinners and parties with... to show off to and family, maybe even strangers. Half of you aren't thinking about being a wife. You just wanna be married. Ask me how I know," she commanded.

When no one spoke up, Kasey answered for herself. "I know because many women will do whatever it takes to get a man without considering what it's going to take to keep him. From attending sporting events to spending time with his mama, going to amusement parks to washing his dirty laundry... then, as soon as she gets him, she makes it very clear nothing she did was officially long-term. And that, ladies, is your Lazarus. Deception, manipulation, and lies all have to be dealt with on the front end. Otherwise, you will reap what you sow on the back end."

It was so quiet a mouse could be heard peeing on a cotton ball.

"Now's the time to ask yourself these questions. If you don't, then let's just get you on over to *Married Life* now because that's exactly where you're gonna end up. In the next room with the 50% who are miserable and the 40% who are maintaining. The choice is yours. Just deal with it... preferably, before you say *I do.*"

Kasey was on a roll. She thought about Kendal, Jason, and Chase. "Just because he asked, doesn't mean God told him to. And, just because you said yes, doesn't mean God told you to either. Neither of you will know until the time comes to roll the stone away, so I suggest taking a long hard look in the mirror and having a long hard conversation with the man you say you want to marry. Because, *Married Life* will be discussing "Let Him Go soon," and I will most assuredly tell you some of you will be needing that class. "And before we move on," Kasey admonished, "just so you know, nearly everyone thinks they're the 10% who might make it."

Chapter 26

"So, what'd you both think about Carmen's news last Friday?" Liz couldn't contain her excitement, and Stony was surprised.

"Wow, Liz. Change of heart?"

"Only since having dinner with Martin. Why do you ask?"

Stony decided now wasn't the time to steal Carmen's thunder. Liz and Martin could wait. "What did I miss?"

"Well," for starters, Jess spoke up, "his family owns an entire chain of restaurants."

"What? Luis?"

"Yeah, Stony, you left in such a hurry we didn't know whether to come after you or to stay and comfort Carmen."

"Comfort Carmen?" Stony was surprised. "Well, you both knew when I last saw Faith and Fletcher, I was a bit out of it and only agreed to meet you because it had been so long since we all hung out."

"I know, but Carmen was so torn between Luis' proposal and her past that she needed help."

As if hearing her name, Carmen rounded the table and took a seat. "Wow, twice in three days."

"Well, only because you bullied us into meeting you again when we left dinner the other night," Jess reminded her. "What's the emergency follow-up for?"

Carmen gave the waitress her lunch order and turned her attention back to her friends who had already ordered. "Well, now that Stony is here, I'd like to ask each of you a favor."

"Well, we know you don't need a loan."

"Ha, ha. Very funny. No, I don't need a loan."

"Good," Stony spoke up. "Word is, Luis is loaded."

Carmen laughed. "Who knew? He only helps out when they're short-staffed."

"Wait. Where was he Friday?" Liz inquired.

Carmen smiled. "That's what I'm trying to tell y'all. He hasn't worked since the night we met."

Stony, Elizabeth, and Jessica gasped. "Are you serious? It's like that?"

"Yes, Stony!" Carmen squeaked. "I met his family about three weeks ago. If you came up from writing every now and again, you'd know that."

"Well, we're not writing, and you didn't tell us."

"Exactly, Jess."

"Liz, I wouldn't tell you anything anyways.

Elizabeth rolled her eyes. Back and forth like teenage girls fighting over makeup brushes, Carmen and Liz were constantly on each other's nerves.

"Get back to the story, please."

"Thank you, Stony," Jess encouraged.

"Well, he took me to meet his family and proposed."

"What? Just like that?"

"Just like that, Liz. Just like that."

"So, it's official. Carmen is getting married.

"Why do you not sound so happy?"

Jess was as surprised by Carmen appearing to be put-off as Stony was. "Okay, so why do you sound so bummed?" she inquired.

Carmen waited to answer until the waitress had left again. Twirling her new engagement ring, she looked Jess in the eyes. "I'm afraid married life won't be as good as single life."

"What on earth would make you think that? You see my relationship with Richard."

"Yeah, but you guys have been in love since college. Not everybody's still happy as long as you two."

"True, but at least give it a try," Jessica encouraged. "I mean, he's a great guy. He's gorgeous, polite, educated..."

"Let's not forget wealthy, Jess," Liz added.

"Yeah, and he's also still a virgin. I mean, Carmen, you hit multiple jackpots," Jessica reassured.

Stony stared at Carmen. Something wasn't right, and she knew it. "Carmen, what's really the reason you're holding back? I mean, Luis is a keeper. By all intended means, you can't do better than him."

Carmen tried to hide her tears. "He loves me."

"Uh, yeah. When's that ever been a reason not to marry?" Liz wanted to know.

Carmen passed on the chance to be sly. Looking at Liz, she responded timidly.

"No man has ever loved me."

"Oh, Carmen..." Liz rushed to her side. "Sweetie, that's because you never required one to." Liz's words simmered in the air. "Even I know dating will get you dinner and holding out will get you diamonds."

Carmen smiled at Liz. "I asked him if he's sur. You know, with the age difference and all... with my past experiences... and he said he'd rather die young with me than be old and have never loved me."

"Awl," Stony and Jess blushed.

"I just needed to be sure he wouldn't change his mind," Carmen admitted. "I mean, I never even realized all my hang-ups until recently."

"Like?"

"Well, Stony, for the first time I remember not feeling loved."

Stony bit into her sandwich and listened to Carmen fill them in on a past they weren't aware of. "Luis came by several months ago and asked me about the photo in my bedroom. The one with me and the group of men."

Vaguely Jessica, Stony, and Liz remembered the night Carmen was in a drunken stupor, and they'd noticed the photo. It was the same night she'd met Luis.

In between chews, Stony asked, "What about it?"

I was about four in that picture. I was surrounded by all of my uncles on my dad's side. At least, I thought they were my uncles... and, I thought he was my dad..." Carmen's voice faded. "That was the last time I remember seeing any of them. I was told they weren't my uncles... he wasn't my father... and the lady on whose lap I sat wasn't my grandma."

The ladies watched Carmen become the four-year-old before their eyes. When tears rolled down her cheeks, it was Liz who passed her a napkin, even though Jessica had told her years prior to let people cleanse. Briefly, she thought back to Jessica's lecture. *When you pass a tissue to someone crying, you're telling them their tears make you uncomfortable. Let them be.* Be that as it may, she was not the therapist.

Carmen continued through faint sobs, "I didn't find out who my real dad was until about four years later. I asked him if he was my dad, and his only answer was 'if I wanted him to be'."

Jessica sipped her raspberry tea and slipped into counseling mode. "Carmen, you do realize that was traumatic shock, right?"

"The only thing I realized," Carmen continued, "was I didn't know who I was; I didn't know who I belonged to. My dad loved me.... Well, the man I thought was my dad loved me. The one I belonged to didn't even want to own me."

"Let me guess," Stony joined the conversation. "And, you've spent your entire life trying to find out where you fit, where you belong?"

"And," Jessica continued, "you've used sex as a means to fill the void, as you've grasped for some form of validation?"

Carmen sat quietly, as Stony and Jessica put pieces of her broken life together. She'd gone from man to man her entire life because she was taken from one who loved her and forced on another who didn't even want her. She'd been pulled away from family who wanted her from birth and was forced to get to know one who didn't know she existed until she was starting third grade.

This time, Jessica stood and joined Carmen at the other side of the table. "Excuse me, Liz."

"Oh, no problem."

Liz traded seats with Jessica, who was in the process of taking Carmen's hand as she sat. Jessica rubbed her fingers across Carmen's shiny new five-karat, emerald cut diamond trio engagement ring. With one karat on each side, the three-karat mound sat in the middle. Jessica tried to lighten the mood. "Good grief, girl. Luis must've sold a leg to pay for this thing."

Carmen smiled softly. "It is beautiful, isn't it?"

"Yes," Jessica confirmed. "And, you deserve it, Carmen."

"And, you deserve him, Carmen," Stony added.

"Carmen, do you realize you have been suppressing all of this inner turmoil your entire life?"

Carmen answered Jessica in her brokenness. "I didn't until recently. It's like he proposed on a Saturday afternoon, and I was crying all Saturday night."

"And, let me guess. They all thought they were tears of joy?" Liz inquired.

Carmen laughed. "Yeah, they did."

"Listen to me, Carmen," Jessica added. "I can understand your hesitation now. It's not that Luis is wealthy. It's not that he wants to marry you. It's not even that you're unsure about him. You're unsure about you."

"Jess is right, Carmen," Stony added. "The four-year-old showed up, and your childhood scars are screaming to heal. If I were you, I wouldn't set a date until they were dealt with."

"I second that one, friend," Jessica agreed. "We've got to help you figure out what happened from four to eight that you've blocked out.

This time, Liz tried to lighten the mood. "Well, look at you just double and triple blessed."

Carmen dabbed the corners of her eyes. "What are you talking about?"

"Good things come in threes. You met a younger man who's never had sex, one. He's wealthy and wants to marry you, two. Your two best friends are therapists, three. It doesn't get any better than that."

The ladies shared a laugh. "Well, at least not until she gets the bill," Jessica threw in.

Carmen shook her head. "Luis will be glad to pay any bill that gets me to the altar."

"Well, I'm proud of you."

"Why is that, Liz?"

"When you met Luis, you were disgusted after the first date."

"That's because he picked me up in the most raggedy car I've ever been in," Carmen explained.

Jessica laughed. "And, let's not forget when you tried to seduce him, and he checked you on it."

"Well, that was hard. I've never been rejected by any man," Carmen continued.

"And, look at you now," Stony beamed. "All grown up and taking responsibility."

"How do you mean?"

"I mean," Stony shared, "you got used to 'the most raggedy car ever' and found out he owns a Bentley."

"Yeah, Carmen, you got used to not having sex and found out he wanted to marry you having never been with you," Jessica added.

"And, you admitted your past is trying to hinder your progress, but you won't let it," Liz stated. "You passed the test, Carmen. You passed a test you didn't even know you were taking and look how it turned out."

Carmen grabbed Liz and gave her a tight squeeze. Liz stood limp and waited for her to let go. Pushing her chair up to the table, Elizabeth smiled. She and Carmen had mended their relationship, and all it took was a heart-to-heart talk with her inner child.

The ladies exited the restaurant together. Carmen had taken the day off to spend time sorting her past. Having lunch with her girls had helped her prepare for her future.

"Same time next week?"

Stony and Jess looked at each other. "Heifer, you just want to get out of coming into the office. You're a client now."

The group laughed. "Same time next week at Mind, Body & Soul. Liz, pencil her in for a joint counseling session with the two of us."

"Confirmed, Stony. I have her down with the both of you for one o'clock next Monday."

Carmen shook her head. "Fine. Just be prepared to spend some time discussing wedding plans."

"We'll discuss wedding plans, when we clear you for marriage."

"Oooohhhh," Liz knew what this meant and couldn't hold it in. "Uhm, yeah, that means you'll be in therapy with the two of them, and then Luis will need to schedule some time with Martin."

Liz was right. She'd worked with Stony enough to know she didn't clear anybody for take-off until both feet were on the ground. Although Carmen would be coming for personal counseling, she couldn't imagine Stony and Jess not going into pre-marital counseling soon after. Right now, Carmen was somewhere between scared stiff and happy as a bear in hibernation. Soon, she'd be fully aware of her conscious self, and when that side of her woke, Stony and Jess would see to it that she and Luis both understood whatever they got is who they would be.

Liz had paid attention over the years and had learned well. Lesson one, if you see him or her and say if only he or she... keep going. Lesson two, if you say he or she would be perfect if... don't look back. Lesson three, if you start to wish he or she didn't... run. Lesson four, if you ever start to think if only I could change... don't stop.

Liz knew Stony and Jess would be sure Carmen was ready long before her wedding day because she needed to be satisfied with herself before she joined anyone else. If Liz hadn't learned anything else from working at MBS, she knew you can't change anybody but yourself and trying was futile.

"Thanks, chicas." Carmen hugged each of her girls once they were outside. "Thanks for reminding me that men who love you won't sleep with you before its time."

"Oh, so you were listening."

"Yes, Jess, I was. Anyone else would have tried, but not Luis. He honors me. For the first time, I know what real love feels like, and it has nothing to do with sex. Intimacy is worth waiting for."

"Awl, she's got it y'all."

"Don't spoil the moment, Liz."

"I'm just saying you learned to respect yourself."

"You're right, I did. I realized I was so busy smiling in the next man's face, I didn't realize the last one had left a price tag on my ass. Everybody saw it but me, until Luis took it off."

"Well, we did."

"Liz?"

"Yes, Carmen."

"I finally like you. Don't blow it."

Liz lowered her head and rocked back and forth on the balls of her feet. Carmen knew she was right.

"Liz?"

"Yeah?"

"Thank you for earning the right to be my bridesmaid. I can confess I never really liked you all that much because you reminded me of who I wanted to be. I was never comfortable with you because you reflected everything I wasn't."

This time, Liz hugged Carmen back. She needed to hear that because she had spent years wondering what she could do to make Carmen like her. Truth was, Carmen didn't like herself. Liz smiled. She was in the wedding, and she had a date.

"Stony, you are my maid of honor. Jess, you're my matron of honor. Any questions?"

Chapter 27

Kasey made her way back to the marriage workshop. So far, her messages to both the singles and those engaged had been well-received. Preparing her thoughts on her next topic, she slowed her pace. She knew those in *Married Life* were ready to hear from the Lord; she just wasn't sure how many were ready to respond to what they heard Him say.

Catching the group up, Kasey gave a synopsis of both the singles and engaged workshops. Once they were on the same page, she began. "I'm going to read verses 38-43. When we get to verse 44, I need you to read aloud with me."

Kasey waited for the pages of the bibles to settle and those using their electronic devices to get logged in before she read the passage she'd stopped short of in her earlier session.

"All together... verse 44... The man who had died came forth, bound hand and foot with wrappings, and his face was wrapped around with a cloth. Jesus said to them, 'Unbind him, and let him go.'"

The ladies took their seats and scooted them closer to their tables. Kasey waited before rendering anymore instructions. "Now that you're all comfy, this will be a quick lesson but a life-long process. In the text, as I've shared with the singles and engaged attendees, Lazarus has died, and Jesus has made his way to Judea. Mary and Martha are both upset at the fact that Jesus wasn't there to keep Lazarus from dying."

Several nods captured Kasey's attention at the table Lola and Kendal shared. "Jesus is now at the tomb of Lazarus, a cave, with a stone lying against it." Kasey stopped. "Now, doesn't that just about sum up marriage?"

Several outbursts of laughter came out. "You ain't lying!" someone yelled.

"No, she's not!" another responded.

Kasey laughed at the audience's exchange. She was sure she would get a few chuckles out of that one. She also knew she needed to keep her presentation as light as she could with this group. With some, she could come out swinging. For others, she would have to tread as if walking on eggshells.

"I won't ask how many of you feel trapped. It's way too early for that."

"Yes, Lord, keep it moving," someone shouted.

"Please do," another chimed in.

"Let's continue," Kasey agreed. She placed her finger in her bible and closed it momentarily. "Now, let's just be honest. We're all married... some happy... others not. True?"

The group divided in head nods and amens. Kasey knew some of them felt like that boulder had been sitting on their chest for years, while others may have only experienced a pebble at the door. If the truth was told, she also knew the group should have been further divided into the haves and the have nots. The haves would have figured out what to throw away and what to keep by now, and the have nots would have figured out nothing is worth holding onto if it's dragging you down. But, despite their different paths, each had ended up in the same place: *The Lazarus Effect.* And, each would be able to either teach or to learn something new in this place. She would not leave until she had done the same.

When the chatter died down over her last question, Kasey asked Glenda for a time check. With 45 minutes to go, she picked back up at the next verse. The ladies followed, as Kasey read. For many, it appeared the section had raised off the page. Silence filled the room, and Kasey asked another question.

"Is it to end in death, or will it be raised?" Kasey watched Kendal. She had been treading lightly in order to build up to her final points. She needed her sister to hear from the Lord concerning Jason and no one else.

Kasey paused once more. "Okay, the singles have to be willing to die. The pre-maritals have to be willing to keep their man from dying, and now we've come to you... the mature, married ladies of the group." Kasey breathed deeply and exhaled. "You ladies have to be willing to make a clear choice. Either let your man, or your idea of marriage, go. But, pay attention," Kasey warned. "Some of you will realize your man isn't the problem; your idea of what your man is supposed to be is."

"I'd pay somebody to take mine," Rita shouted.

"I've been trying to get rid of mine for years," another added.

Kasey smiled. For every woman who had joked about her husband getting lost, she knew there was a husband who had already been found. These two were no exception.

"What's your name?" Kasey inquired of the first.

"Me?"

"Yes." Kasey pointed to the lady sitting with Kendal and Lola.

"Margo Rita," the lady responded shyly.

“How much would you be willing to pay?” The crowd burst into laughter. Kasey waved her arms to quiet the ladies. “Seriously, how much? Because, I can assure you, someone on the other side of that door... down the hall in the singles conference... would love to have him.”

The ladies settled down. Kasey returned to the last verse after giving each of them something to think about. “If you turn your attention to the 44th verse, as you can see, Lazarus comes forth and is still bound... with hand and foot wrappings, a head wrap—and that’s not a hairdo wrap, Kasey added for emphasis trying to take the sting out of the room—and Jesus spoke one last time, unbind him and let him go. Repeat after me, let him go.”

“Let him go,” the ladies faintly whispered. The ceiling fan hummed louder than the group who had started out livelier. Kasey thought about that rat peeing on a cotton ball and smiled. She had their undivided attention. They were now fully aware of the room full of single ladies looking for a husband.”

Having spoken, Kasey divided the ladies into several groups. She doubted, once more, she’d be invited back again. It was actually quite interesting how all of this had turned out. Had it not been for her twin, she would’ve had the typical message heard across almost every other ministry platform: pray and praise your way through.

However, she had spent the last few months with her sister going through marital problems and a love triangle. *Some things you just never imagine yourself in,* Kasey internalized. *It's funny how God has His own way of getting each of our attention.*

"Repeat after me, I'm free to love myself and to embrace my future," she encouraged.

The ladies were louder this time around, as they repeated Kasey's affirmation.

"He who finds a wife finds a good thing," say it.

The ladies followed suit.

"Did we say he who finds a *woman*?"

Kasey heard many *nos* and received many nods. "Right. Just as I shared with the engaged ladies, we have to accept that some of us are mad at our husbands for not finding what he was looking for."

Kasey retold several lessons she'd shared with the earlier group from a different perspective. She was once single, had been engaged and was now married. She understood each season for different reasons and was now compelled to make sure no one else lost themselves trying to find someone else.

"Ladies, this isn't going to be easy," Kasey warned. "But, I promise, if you want to go where God is trying to take you, move without haste, and don't look back. From today on, don't look back."

Many people shifted in their seats. "Proverbs 18:22 clearly states, 'he who finds a wife finds a good thing and obtains favor from the Lord.'"

"That's right!" someone shouted.

The energy was returning, but Kasey knew it was short-lived. "Who amongst us can say that applies to their husband?"

Not a single hand remained down. Even Lola and Kendal participated. "Thank you all," Kasey continued. "If it was only you and I, privately, in this room... and I told you I see you... I know you... and I am aware you were looking for a father and not a family, how would you answer this next question."

Kasey felt the stares. "Help me, Lord. Make it clear. By a show of hands, if you could do it over again would you do it differently?" Slowly, a few hands went up here and there. "Thank you; thank you very much for your honesty."

This was the group Kasey knew would benefit most. Those who were honest with themselves and everyone else. Those who acknowledged they had daddy issues they'd hoped "Danny" would fix but had failed to do so.

Now, they were angry and bitter or afraid and insecure, if not all.

"Those of you who raised your hands, please come to the center and stand with me." Kasey waited for each to arrive. "Don't be shy. If you raised your hand, please come."

In a crowd as large as this one, she knew there would be slim pickings of those who wanted change badly enough to create it, so Kasey continued to encourage each one as they made their way down. "Thank you, ladies, for joining me. Please take a seat."

Kasey sat at the head table with her guests. "We will attempt to share, in open dialogue, what transparency looks like, feels like, and is capable of. Repeat after me; I am moving on."

The crowd repeated.

"No, no. This is for the those at the table. The ones who were brave enough to acknowledge their truth. Those of you who are trying to convince everyone else it's all good, keep trying."

The audience murmured.

"Ladies, please repeat after me," Kasey continued. "I am moving on."

The group sitting with her complied.

"If I want to move forward, it would be selfish of me to keep holding him back."

The ladies at the table echoed Kasey's words, as the others looked on and listened in.

Looking into the crowd, Kasey acknowledged the rest of the group again. She walked back to the podium and spoke to all of them. "It is not right to keep people bound by our *illegitimate* expectations. We do not get to put our burdens off on someone else and blame them for not carrying them."

The group stared in silence as Kasey explained her stance. "You two, come here." Kasey waited for the ladies to join her. "If I put 10 bricks in your arms, without asking, do I have a right to expect you to carry them?"

"Uh, no!" the participant exclaimed.

Kasey turned to the other. "Okay, if I ask her to carry 10 bricks, and *she* says yes, does she have a right to expect *you* to help her?"

The second lady shook her head. "No, she doesn't. I might, but she doesn't have the right to expect it."

"Thank you, both."

As the ladies returned to their seats, Kasey went on. "Why do we think we have a right to shape our husbands? Trust if he isn't who you want him to be when you meet him, he surely won't become who you want him to be just because you marry him."

The silence grew thicker, and Kasey continued. "How do you know if this applies to you? Great question. Thanks for asking," Kasey entertained the dialogue with herself for the benefit of all of her guests. "The answer is, if you have more marriage than you have moments, what you have is a mess no one wants to help you carry... including your man. Your expectations have outlived your happily ever after, and in many cases, he is outta there."

Lola's eyes brightened, and she beamed, proud the woman standing before them was her daughter.

"Marriage is calculated in years; moments are calculated in time. Hear me, ladies. Time does not equate to tenure in a relationship. You can be married 50 years and not have a single moment worth remembering." The crowd gasped and Kasey went on. "Capture more moments because if you've got more years together than you have been making memories together, you don't have a marriage. You had a wedding."

"Well, finally, somebody said it."

A single-person applause echoed. Kasey looked up from the stage and out into the audience. Making no distinction between who was clapping and who wasn't, she turned her attention back to the ladies at her table and acknowledged the woman who had been silent with a smile and a nod.

"Rita, what would you say if I told you to show up for yourself and stop putting expectations on your husband to do things your way? Do it *yourself*," Kasey stressed. Looking out into the crowd, she went on. "What if I said let your husband be who his mama and daddy gave birth to, and whatever God intended... whether you like it or not? What if I told you to be truly happy, you have to let go of your husband and grab onto God?"

Stunned, Margo Rita rambled. "I... I don't know."

"And, that's perfectly alright," Kasey assured and kept her private thoughts to herself about the woman who was ready to sell her husband to the highest bidder earlier.

"I can help her," the clapping-stranger offered.

"Okay, take a stab at it," Kasey accepted.

"For starters, I'd tell her he likes his eggs over-easy and his bacon cooked in the oven. I'd remind her he hates clutter and insists on flat sheets, not fitted. I'd tell her what drives her insane about him, makes my heart flutter. I'd tell her to let him go and don't run and tell her mama he left her for me. He left her for himself."

Rita stood and reached across the table when she recognized her husband's mistress behind the shades and a wig. With the group at the table restraining both, Rita spewed verbal insults as Jaiden rushed from the audience to her rescue.

"You have some nerve! What are you even doing here?"

"Yes, what are you doing here? If what I am gathering is true, then you are not married," Kasey interjected.

"No, I'm not married. My mother just thought it would be a good idea if instead of the singles workshop I attended the marriage one. She thought it would be good for me to put myself in the other woman's shoes."

"She must've wanted you to *feel* the other woman's shoes," Rita retorted.

"Excuse me," Kasey walked over to the stranger. "What is your name?"

"Her name is Ratchet," Rita screamed. "Ratchet Ass Rachel."

Rita struggled to free herself from the grips of the other ladies around the table. "She came for an ass whoopin', and I'm gonna give her one. Let me go!"

"Calm down," Jaiden urged. "Calm down."

"*Calm* down? Calm *down*? She brought her skank ass into a marriage workshop she knew I would be attending and manipulated her way onto the stage, and you're telling me to calm down?"

Rachel smirked, as security made their way inside with Glenda. "It's okay. I heard what I needed to hear... Somebody say to all y'all wanna-be-married women, who have no intention of ever becoming a wife, let him go."

Although that wasn't Kasey's final word on the matter, Rachel had hit her target.

"Actually, Rachel, it was for the purposes of perusing God's highest calling. You let him go, and grab hold to *Him.* A husband is merely "a man." We must get a grip, calm down, take control, and come to ourselves for *the* Man."

Rachel singlehandedly applauded once more. Rolling her eyes at Rita, she nodded at Kasey. "Like she said, let him go. He didn't leave you for me. He left you for him."

As security was preparing to escort Rachel out, Kasey stopped them. Sensing the woman felt she had won, Kasey wanted to be sure she understood. "Wait. A man isn't settling when he chooses his family, Rachel."

"No, but he is when he chooses his non-wife, wife for the sake of the family."

Rachel eyed Rita again. Kasey sensed there was more to be told. "Rita, I know this is probably the last place you wanted all of this aired. However, sometimes, God does the unexpected. Your marriage appears to be in the midst of a storm. See this as the umbrella."

Kasey took a deep breath. This was the moment of truth, "Rita, did your husband leave you for this woman?"

A single tear left one of her eyes. Margo Rita reflected on the last five years of her life. When she thought about their memories, few were worth holding on to. Now, if she could start again, she would. She loved her husband; she'd just hated being his wife and everything she couldn't change about him the first year. "No. He didn't leave me for her."

Kasey walked to her side and whispered in Jaiden's ear. "Take her across the hall."

Looking at Rita, Kasey sympathized. "You cry long, and you cry hard. When you're done, never cry over that thing again."

Gloria assisted the two ladies and security attempted to remove Rachel. While one would never return, Kasey knew the other would never be the same. Although Rita hated to admit it, Kasey knew Rachel was right. Her husband had left for himself. Rachel was simply the deciding factor; now, Rita would have to choose to let him be who he was with someone else.

"God hates divorce," some shouted.

Cheers and applause supported the woman's claim.

"Yes, he does, Rachel retaliated. But, it is still an option. Your Boaz could be waiting around the corner, but most of you are too afraid or insecure to go check. Stop holding onto Bobby! God ain't pleased by that either."

"Bobby?"

The crowd whispered and Kasey was confused.

"Excuse me, Bobby? Is that Rita's husband's name?"

Again, Rachel smirked. "No, his name is Gerald. Bobby is who most of these women settle for instead of pursuing Boaz. Then, they're mad because Bobby is his best self with someone like me. If you let "Bobby" go, then Lazarus will sleep."

Kasey hadn't anticipated such a finale; however, Rachel must've read her notes on the way out. Eying the crowd, there was really nothing else to say. Kasey swallowed, as Rachel was being escorted out, and Jaiden was across the hall struggling to console a now overwhelmed Rita. Finding Kendal and Lola in the crowd, she smiled softly and blinked away her own tears. "Unbind him and let him go... and see the glory of God."

Chapter 28

Stony took a break before starting her next chapter. So much was packed into that last one, she didn't know what else needed to be said. From "letting him go" to "he might come back," she was stuck mentally fighting for Kendal, but tending to Kasey.

Entering her username and password on the laptop, she waited for the desktop to appear. She typed the first words that came to mind when MS Word launched.

"Dinner is ready," Hayden announced to Kasey, Lola, and Kendal.

When the ladies took their seats at the table, Hayden blessed the food and waited for someone to fill him in. When no one spoke, he asked.

"So, how did it go?"

"Before or after the fight?"

Hayden delayed putting his fork into his mouth. Eying his wife, he waited. "After."

"Good choice," Lola informed.

"Why is that, Mother?"

Lola looked at Kasey and then turned to Kendal. "Because, whatever caused it need not be mentioned."

"Interesting concept, Lola." Hayden stared at his mother-in-law, sister-in-law, and wife respectively. Each returned a blank stare. "Lola, what happened?"

"Well, why on earth did you ask me?"

The twang of her sentence lingered. Hayden knew she was nervous when she slowed her speech and dragged her answers to that degree.

"Because, you're the most direct."

Lola laughed. "Is that your way of calling these two liars?"

Kasey and Kendal raised their heads. When their eyes met, each laughed at Lola's candidness. "Well, I guess that sums it up," Kasey answered.

Lola looked across the table at Hayden. "Do you really want to know what happened?"

"That's why I asked *you*," he reiterated.

"Well, some single woman decided it was a good idea to crash a married women's workshop."

"Knowledge is knowledge, Lola. She must be preparing for her own marriage."

"Oh, she was preparing alright. She was preparing for an ass whipping," Kendal shared.

Hayden coughed after taking a bite of his breadstick. “Excuse me?”

Kasey decided to take over the conversation before her mother and sister choked her husband any further. “It would appear one of the conference attendees is involved with another attendee’s husband.”

Squinting his eyes, Hayden tried to understand.

“I know,” Kasey shook her head. “Hard to believe the boldness of some people.”

Hayden wiped the corners of his mouth and swallowed.

“And, she had the nerve to get up there and tell that man’s wife the very things she loves about him are the very things she, on the other hand, hates,” Lola added.

Hayden tried to keep the “she’s” separate. “You mean the girlfriend told the wife what she, herself, loves about him that she, the wife, hates?”

“Exactly. Just tacky,” Kendal added. “When did side chicks become so bold?”

“When reality TV made it cute to be ratchet,” Hayden assumed.

Lola laughed out loud. “Ha! Ratchet Ass Rachel!”

Kendal and Kasey looked at their mother. Lola was patting the table with her fist, and Hayden was lost. "That woman said, 'Ratchet As..."

"Mother, we were there," Kasey interrupted.

"What is she talking about?" Hayden inquired.

"Kasey asked the mistress her name, and the wife said Ratchet Ass Rachel," Kendal explained.

Lola burst into both tears and laughter. Wiping her eyes on a napkin, she tried to compose herself before letting go again.

"Well, Honey, welcome to the world of marriage counseling." This time, Hayden laughed. Neither Kendal nor Kasey joined him, and Lola was still drying her tears from before.

"Why is that funny?" Kasey wanted to know.

"Because, I keep telling people for every woman who hates the sound of her man taking a breath, there is a woman waiting for the next phone call to simply hear him breathe. And, she's asking him why he even goes home."

Hayden cut into the remainder of his steak. The ladies sat in silence. By now, Lola had calmed down. When he looked up, he noticed their blank stares. "I didn't say it's right. I simply said it's real. So real that apparently this one decided to ask his wife. Again, I'm not saying it's right. But, it is very much real."

Kendal helped Kasey with the dishes when they were done eating, and Lola cleared the table. Hayden's words had struck a chord neither of them wanted to hear. When everything was clean and tidy, each said good night and headed for bed.

Lola sat on the ottoman and removed her shoes. She knew all too well a parent is only as happy as their saddest child, and a mature woman is only as happy as her man... if she truly loves him. She knew while Kasey struggled to keep a healthy balance between her role as first lady and wife, Kendal struggled to simply keep afloat. The marriage workshop had been more than enough information without the additional drama of Margo Rita and Rachet Rachel. When Lola replayed their exchange, she laughed again. "Ha! Ratchet Ass Rachel!" Lola laughed so loudly at herself that she didn't hear Kasey knock.

"Are you okay in there?"

"Yes, I'm fine. Check on your sister."

"That's where I'm headed now. Get some rest. I love you," Kasey spoke through the cracked door.

"I love you, too. You did well, Kasey. You did well. Good night."

"Good night, Mother."

Kasey closed the door and made her way down the hallway to the other guest room. While she knew Kendal was preparing for sleep, she had no idea Lola was on the brink of surrender.

"Hey," Kasey knocked and entered.

"Hey."

"Long day, huh?"

Kendal smiled. "Yeah, but it was worth it."

"Yeah, it was." Kasey sat on the side of the bed next to her sister. "How are you holding up?"

Kendal reflected in silence. "We would appear to be keeping it together fairly well if we didn't have to sleep together."

"Well," Kasey continued, "maintain as long as you can."

Kendal laughed. "Well, I'm not sure what 'as long as I can' looks like. What does that mean anyway?"

"It means, things aren't always as they seem, Kendal. Make the best of it until God gives you His final say."

"I'm not for keeping up a charade. And, in the meantime, who am I going to make love to?" Kendal wanted to know.

"What? What do you mean?"

Kendal waited before responding. After a few moments of silence, she spoke. "I can't bring myself to be with him anymore. First, I thought it was me. Then, I thought it was the baby. Now, I know it's absolutely me."

"But, how?"

"Kasey, I have tried. When he touches me, I cringe. I'm tired of going through the motions. I can't see past him and Simoné being together. The very idea that he was with her turns my stomach."

"Kendal, are you still throwing up after you make love?"

"If you want to call it that. Yes."

Kasey covered her sister's hand in her own. "I'm sorry."

"I don't know what for. You didn't do anything."

"No, but I can't even imagine what you're going through. To have gone from hanging the stars over your man's head to watching every single flicker go out... I just can't imagine."

Kasey tried to conceal her lie. She had as much of a clue as Lola did. After a few distant memories resurfaced, Kasey spoke.

“Kaye, do you remember my high school sweetheart?”

Kendal paused for a moment. She wanted to be sure before responding.

“Yeah. Jessie, right?”

“Yes, Jessie.”

Kendal looked confused. “What’s he got to do with anything?” She stood in irritation. “You’d better not tell me you’re sleeping with that boy again!”

Kasey laughed. “Not in his dreams.”

““Well?”

“Well, what?”

“Well, why did you bring him up?”

Kasey placed both hands in her lap, after tucking a strand of hair behind one ear.

“Remember when I used to spend the night over at their house?”

Kendal chuckled. “Remember? How could I forget? When every boy within a five-mile radius found out you got to sleep at Jessie’s house the phone rang nonstop.”

The two reflected on the memories of their sophomore year in high school. Kasey had made the cheer squad, and Kendal was busy with band. She’d been asked out more times than she could remember, but she blew everyone off. Kendal had always been focused on her goals, and boys were an added benefit that was also an endless commodity. She had the rest of her life to be involved. However, she only had now to get it together.

Kendal lowered her head, and Kasey took notice. "What's wrong, Kaye?"

"I seemed to have it all together all my life. Now..." Kendal shrugged and sighed. "Now, everything's fallen apart."

"Listen to me, Kendal." Kasey looked her twin straight in her eyes. "You have nothing to be ashamed of. Do you hear me? Nothing."

Kendal looked up. "Yes, I do. I've always had a plan. I just never planned "my plan" wouldn't succeed. I've always believed if I worked hard, and I didn't give up, I could do anything."

"You can and you have, Kendal." Kasey reassured.

"Yeah, well, nobody ever told me that as long as I did my part God would not do His."

Kasey paused. Kendal had stumped her, but she understood. "Kendal," Kasey coaxed, "God always has a purpose and a plan. His plans never fail... Remember when I spent my last night over at Jessie's?"

"Vaguely," Kendal replied.

Her demeanor had changed. Kendal's sprit had been broken, and Kasey wondered if this was really the time to tell her story. She needed to, but not for reasons she previously considered. She needed to because Kendal needed to know sometimes life simply wasn't fair, and it was okay.

"What I never told you guys is that when Pastor Rudolph left for work in the evenings, Lady Joyce let Jessie and I sleep together."

Kendal raised her head. Her eyes wandered from the stained mahogany wood floor to the ceiling, then rested on Kasey.

"Are you telling me the First Lady let you and Jessie lay up? Together? In the Pastor's house?"

Kasey said nothing. She could tell Kendal was processing it all mentally. Soon after, Kendal broke her silence with a hearty laugh. Squealing, she could hardly contain herself.

"Oh, my gosh. Talk about keeping up the charade!" Kasey sat and waited for Kendal to calm down. When she pulled it together, Kasey continued. "Well, I'm glad you think it's funny now. I don't."

"Oh, come on, Kasey. You had to think this was funny... and a bit ironic."

"Had... like in the past... Yes. I did think it was funny, then. Now, not so much."

Kendal watched her sister. Kasey had grown into a beautiful woman. They were grateful to still have her after the scare she'd given them years earlier.

"Kendal, the last time I stayed with Jessie, something happened I've never spoken of."

Kendal took note of Kasey's tone. "I'm listening."

"As usual, we ate dinner at seven o'clock, and Pastor Rudolph said his goodbyes. Around 10:00 PM we said our goodnights and went to Jessie's room. At 5:00 AM the next morning, Lady Joyce always woke me. She said Pastor got off at 5:00 AM and would be home by 5:30."

"Okay, what's unusual about that?" Kendal inquired. "I mean, aside from the fact that First Lady let you lay up."

"Well, the last time when I got home, mom had this look on her face. Like maybe she'd been up all night. I'd seen that look many times, but for some reason, it was more prevalent then... like she was zoned out. I hugged and kissed her, but she seemed so cold... distant. I showered and got dressed, as usual. By then you were usually up, and we'd sit and just watch her. This time, however, I did the opposite. I turned on the shower and stood in the hallway. I could hear mom and dad. He'd been out all night again. I thought she was worried about me, but she had been up all night again because of him. Mom didn't know who; she just knew there was someone. She'd known for months."

Kendal sat quietly. "Dad was seeing someone?"

"Yes, he was. And, Mother knew it."

"But, how? Why?"

Kasey cleared her throat. "Us."

"Us? What do you mean, us?"

"I overheard Dad tell Mom she ignores him. She never has time for him anymore."

"How could he say that? She had time to sit up all night worried about him, but he only saw what he wanted to, apparently."

Kendal was furious. No wonder she'd married Jason. He was just like her lying, cheating, conniving, manipulating, and no good father. She stood. "Well, that says a lot."

"That's not all, Kendal."

Kendal laughed. "Not all? What more could you possibly tell me?"

Kasey continued. "After noticing Mom's behavior over the next few days, it became apparent that something was going on. So, I decided to pay further attention."

"Well, what more did you see, and why didn't you say anything to me?"

"I wanted to be sure... I saw enough to decide to test a theory, and I didn't need to tell you and be wrong."

"What did you do?"

"The next time I went to Jessie's, I willed myself to stay awake until he fell asleep. Dad had dropped me off and left, Pastor had eaten dinner and said goodnight, so we went to bed, and I waited."

"For what?"

"For Dad to come and get me."

"What? That doesn't make any sense, Kasey."

"Neither did him always being there at 5:00 AM when Lady Joyce woke me." Kasey spoke through clenched teeth. In silence, both sat momentarily.

"What happened next, Kase?"

"At midnight, Lady Joyce answered the phone. She always talked to Pastor on his break and went to bed. He always called when he worked overnight at the electric company."

"That sounds normal."

Kasey smiled at her sister's innocence. "She called someone else as soon as she closed her bedroom door."

"Are you saying Lady Joyce called Dad, Kasey?"

"No. Don't really think I can say that and prove it."

Kasey tapped her fingernails against her cheek with one hand like she was still trying to connect the dots after all the years gone by. "But, I will say this." She paused. "He came back. A little after midnight, he came back."

Kendal's eyes watered like the 15-year-old girl she once was. She'd known for years her father had been involved with someone else on some level. He hadn't just cheated their mother; he'd cheated her and Kasey, as well.

"Lady Joyce? Dad was sleeping with First Lady Joyce?"

Kendal tried to erase the thought from her mind. She held her breath and released the frustration that had brewed. "And, Mom didn't know?"

"Mom knew nothing about Lady Joyce, Kendal. Neither did she know Dad used me to get out."

For the second time that day, Kasey blinked away her own tears. She'd called Lola Mom several times since she'd begun. Willing herself not to shed another tear, she cleared her throat. "No, Kendal, Mom doesn't know... and it's my fault."

No longer able to hide her emotions, Kasey let the tears fall. "It's my fault."

Kendal took her seat beside Kasey again. This time, it was her turn to do the soothing. "Kase, this isn't your fault. It's not your fault." Kendal understood why Kasey had blamed herself. She just wished she had known that she did. Their sophomore year had started out as a dream. By Christmas, it had become a nightmare.

"Kasey, I know I don't say it much, but I'm proud of the woman you are. You're wiser and stronger now, and I'm just glad you're my best friend and sister, too." Kasey squeezed Kendal back when she hugged her. Kendal was also glad Kasey had managed to find herself. She'd watched her sister lose sight of who she was in the midst of their parents' struggle. She had poured herself into school, but Kasey had rebelled. She broke up with Jessie, started drinking and abusing drugs. It was during that time when she had been rushed to ER. They thought they would lose Kasey, but their mom had internally died instead.

Kendal had known people who had been hurt by churches and pastors who had lost themselves. They didn't have faith in Christ, only in people. When the people had disappointed them, in this case Lady Joyce and Dad, their hope had died. Kendal had never placed her hope in any natural man... at least not until Jason. Now, she understood all too well.

"Thanks, Kase."

"For what?"

"For telling me. My children will always come first. They deserve to have me whole; they deserve to see me healed."

Kasey smiled. "You're welcome."

Kendal had gotten it. She knew a woman could only truly love one man from her soul and the core of her being. Chase had been born there. Jason had been planted.

Kasey interrupted the silence, "You okay, Kendal?"

Kendal nodded and wiped away a single tear. "I am. I just have to fight my way through the loneliness of motherhood—for the sake of my children. I have to do the next right thing…for everyone."

Although she had no children of her own, Kasey understood. Her father had left her mother and returned; now, Jason had done the same. Somehow, she knew what Kendal was thinking. Lola had lost her will to fight, but Kendal had found her reason to live.

It wasn't a charade; it was merely a choice. It was a sacred kind of love.

The Finale:
Beautiful Lies

"New message from Chase Alexander," the phone announced. Kendal washed and dried her hands on the dish towel hanging over her shoulder.

Entering her password, she wondered what could be so important that Chase had reached out to her. It had been months since either had spoken directly; however, Kasey had delivered several "hellos" on his behalf.

Kendal clicked the hyperlink in the text and waited for YouTube to open. When the video appeared, the corners of her mouth softly turned upward. As Mariah Carey belted you will always be my baby, her eyes misted. Chase hadn't typed not one single word; he'd only copied and pasted the video link to a song that would now hold as special a place in her heart as he did.

"Mommy, are you crying?"

Kendal turned to face Julie. "Only happy tears."

"Well, you've cried a lot lately."

Kendal patted her face dry with the dish towel she'd dried her hands on earlier. While it may not have been the most sanitary thing she could find, it was the closest.

"I know, Julie. Mommy's going through a tough time right now."

"Okay, but if you keep crying you're not gonna have any tears left."

Kendal suddenly burst into laughter. "I guess what they say is true."

"What?" Julie inquired.

"Kids really do say the darnedest things," Kendal answered while pulling her daughter into her arms.

Julie squealed with laughter, as Jason walked in with the boys. "Hey, what am I missing?"

"Mommy crying happy tears."

"Happy tears?" asked Jacob.

"What are those?" Joshua wanted to know.

Kendal laughed again. "It's when you're not crying because you're sad, but because you're happy,"

Jason answered his inquisitive son. Jason took notice that Kendal seemed to be enjoying herself. She hadn't laughed in a long while, and he wished it could go on forever, he had learned the hard way forever isn't promised to anyone.

"So, what am I missing out on?" he wanted to know.

Kendal pulled the twins into her squeeze-hug with Julie. Pretending she could hug them all so hard they would pop, she gritted her teeth and growled while softly tickling them individually.

"No! Nooo!" Julie laughed, as Kendal held onto her. "Stop! Let go. Le'go, mommy!"

Laughing, Kendal released them all. She hadn't intended to ignore Jason's question; she just didn't want the moment interrupted.

"Just making memories," Kendal shared. "Soon, I won't be able to do as much physically."

Kendal rubbed her stomach. Jason watched and smiled. She was glowing and the now protruding basketball-shaped belly she had once questioned God about was the center of her focus. He wanted to hug her and kiss the top of her head, but still she limited her activity with him. Instead, he watched her continued interaction with the kids and enjoyed the memories being made.

"Need any help with dinner?"

It had been a while since Kendal had made it home in time to eat with the family, and tonight she had decided to cook. Jason knew there were times she'd purposely worked late to avoid him. However, she was always intentional about arriving before the children were put to bed.

“No, you can all go wash up. By the time you return, the table will be set.”

Jason disappeared with the children, and Kendal reflected on more memorable times. She hadn’t been the best person to keep company with since returning from Kasey’s but, if she went back even farther, she hadn’t really been the best company since returning from Chicago. She had tried to put everything in its proper place and keep things in perspective; she just hadn’t planned on finding out about the pregnancy. With the three children they already had, she was prepared to leave Jason. With the news of a fourth child, she felt obligated to stay.

Waiting for her family to return for dinner, Kendal rehashed eight months of conversations. From talking to herself in the bathroom mirror to hanging up on her sister, she tried to hide the burden she felt trying to keep it altogether. Having initially spoken with Jason and Chase separately, she wanted to reveal all that was tearing her apart to each.

As the children’s voices made their way into the kitchen before their little bodies did, Kendal placed the last cup of juice on Julie’s tray. She’d spend the last few weeks thinking about Kasey's marriage workshop and reflecting on her father's affair. *Surely, this isn't what life is all about.*

Jason rounded the corner as Kendal's thoughts faded and made his way to the table. Grabbing her hand, he asked the children to do the same with one another. When the circle was complete, he blessed the food and his family. In the silence just before the 'amen,' Kendal's phone chimed again.

"New message from Chase Alexander."

Beautiful Lies will conclude the series. To be notified when the book debuts, sign up at **www.StonyRhodes.com!**

Review Request

Thank you for purchasing and reading my book. I am extremely grateful you took this journey with me and hope you were not only entertained but truly found value in reading it. **Please keep the momentum and support going and consider sharing with friends or family and leaving a review online.** Your review means a lot, and your feedback and support are always appreciated and allow me to continue doing what I love… *Writing!*

Again, thank you for being the greatest part of my story. By the way, if you read Book One, you can also review *Second Time Around* if you haven't had a chance. (Family and friends, I'm serious. Before you text me, head on over to Amazon and review now.)

Appreciation

It took a team effort to bring this project to pass. Without certain individuals, I might still be procrastinating.

I send a special thank you to friends and to family, who allow me the time and opportunity to grow as a writer…an artist! I get to create something beautiful that inspires (and entertains) other readers and writers alike.

Now, to the group of individuals who read advanced copies and shared your insight, some of whom have been waiting on this book for years, thanks for making yourselves available and for the valuable feedback that was necessary for this second story to come together. Your involvement in this project was the culmination of many nights (and some days) of solid work and faithful service. Thank you for seeing the value in it.

Shaundale

About the Author

Stony Rhodes is an international award-winning fiction writer, who seeks to empower those in transition through colorful stories of desperation and contempt. Mid-life doesn't have to be a crisis, and choices don't necessarily have to come from chaos…

But just in case it is (or they do)…

I've spent the past decade in a state of metamorphosis and now enjoy the freedom that comes from being transparent. As they say, "What gets covered doesn't heal," and as a mental health advocate, I realize that this is the time for each of us who have grown weary of always being strong, always being brave, and always going along to get along to do what we need to do and take better care of ourselves. We must stop the cycle of "never have time for me."

Life happens. It keeps on "lifing."

Yeah, life is gonna life!

But, we need a safe place to land, and if the world isn't going to give us one, then "by golly" I'm creating one—

through stories of laughter, love, and a little bit of don't give a shit. (Took me 45 years to start cussing.)

Let's make it work for us!

Let's find ourselves, use our voices, and proclaim our peace! Mental health is real. Depression is real. Divorce is real. But don't separate from yourself to hold somebody (or something) else together. **Read that again!** Do not fall apart, trying to hold somebody or something else together. *Nah!*

We're not doing that anymore!

XOXO!

www.ingramcontent.com/pod-product-compliance
Lightning Source LLC
LaVergne TN
LVHW091116080826
845145LV00008B/1935

* 9 7 8 0 9 7 7 7 2 4 5 1 2 *